THANKSGIVING DADDY

BY
RACHEL LEE

D0318093

MILLS
BOON®

First published in Great Britain 2013
by Mills & Boon, an imprint of Harlequin (UK) Limited,
Eton House, 18-24 Paradise Road, Richmond, Surrey TW9 1SR

© Susan Civil-Brown 2013

ISBN: 978 0 263 90160 3

23-1113

Harlequin (UK) policy is to use papers that are natural, renewable and recyclable products and made from wood grown in sustainable forests. The logging and manufacturing processes conform to the legal environmental regulations of the country of origin.

Printed and bound in Spain
by Blackprint CPI, Barcelona

"Am I still a challenge?"

"You're carrying my son inside of you. How could you not be a challenge? But you're still sexy as hell."

Edie swore quietly.

"Sorry," Seth said. "If you don't like peeks inside my head, don't ask."

She faced him then. "You know, Seth Hardin, you're driving me nuts. We can't have a discussion like this on a public street."

He pointed. "Half a block that way."

She started marching quick time, looking for all the world as if she were on parade, back stiff, strides even and firm. He kept up without difficulty.

"Don't get breathless," he said.

"Oh, shut up."

He almost grinned. No more eggshells, at least for now. The gloves were off.

Conard County: The Next Generation

Rachel Lee was hooked on writing by the age of twelve and practiced her craft as she moved from place to place all over the United States. This *New York Times* best-selling author now resides in Florida and has the joy of writing full-time.

To my babies, all grown now. I'm so proud of you.

Prologue

Flying with the air force combat search and rescue team had given Major Edith Clapton nerves of steel. At least when she was in the middle of all hell breaking loose. This op had been like many other ops, flying into enemy territory to pull out a recon unit, this time a group of navy SEALs. She didn't want to know their mission. None of her business. Her job was to fly that Pave Hawk helicopter in and pull them out no matter how dangerous it became.

This time there had been gunfire and rocket-propelled grenades, enough to put her teeth on edge, especially during the part where she had to hover over a cliff top that simply didn't seem big enough, getting far closer than she would have liked, given her rotors.

It had been close, but there had been wounded in the team she was picking up, one of whom needed a litter, and under fire there was no way she could use a rope lift. They needed to be in and out as fast as possible, with minimal exposure to those attackers on the surrounding mountains.

So trying to hover while nearly scraping the ground of a nearby cliff, holding perfectly still while fire came her way…well, it might take some time to calm down completely. The nerves of steel that helped her on missions never failed to desert her back at the base.

After showering, she headed to the officers' club, looking for a good meal and an illicit drink or two. Illicit because legally no alcohol was allowed in Afghanistan, but somehow it made its way in to the bases anyway.

She drank only after a mission, and only a couple of drinks. There were too many others around her to remind her that alcohol could become a crutch. She didn't want any crutches, but she did want to wind down. Every nerve and muscle in her body seemed to be shrieking.

She nodded to the people she knew, which was nearly every officer at this base, and found herself a rickety table in the corner. They were supposedly at the rear of all the fighting, but that could change at any moment. In the meantime, this clone of the U.S. tried to pass for normal, with hurriedly built structures, a few fast-food joints and an exchange.

It didn't quite deceive anyone, but it was sure better than some of the firebases she had seen. For some, spending time here almost amounted to a vacation.

She saw the SEAL team walk in just as she was being served a steak. Yeah, a real steak. It hardly seemed fair when so many of her fellow troops would be dining on barely warmed freeze-dried rations tonight. It was, however, one of the perks of being stationed at a permanent base. Well, semipermanent. She let the politics of it all fly by her.

She was on her second drink and halfway through her steak when one of the SEALs she had rescued pulled out a chair and sat across from her.

"Mind?" he asked.

"We're not supposed to hang," she reminded him.

Like many of his type, he seemed to be all hard angles and planes encased in muscle. Short dark hair, brown eyes that held flecks of green. Just sitting there, he looked dangerous.

"No one knows you pulled us out today. Besides, if we can't trust the people in this room, who can we trust?" He stuck out his hand. "Seth Hardin."

She shook it, taking in the subdued captain's eagle, which was stitched into the collar of his camouflage uniform. His rank was the naval equivalent of the air force's colonel. "Edith Clapton."

"That was some flying job you did out there," he said.

"Thanks. Your guys okay?"

"One just got winged. We're still waiting to hear about the other. Your medics probably saved his life."

That was the other part of the job: she extracted, but in the rear of her helicopter she carried the bare bones of an emergency medical team when it was needed. Today it had been needed. They'd done some stripping in the cabin to make room. "That's what we do."

He smiled faintly. "Doesn't mean I can't be grateful."

The waiter, a civilian working for a contractor, came over to take his order. He wanted a steak, too, and a couple of beers.

"Time to forget," he said.

She couldn't agree more. There'd be another mission, tomorrow or the next day, but for right now it was time to play the mental game of "everything's normal and okay." And maybe it was, as much as it could be in the middle of a war.

"Let me buy you another drink," he said. "It's the least I can do."

"I usually limit myself to two."

A sparkle came into his green-brown eyes. "Usually. Maybe tonight is different. It's just one more. I don't want to give you a hangover."

She hesitated, then said, "Thanks." Another whiskey. More wind-down. Just this once. Maybe it would quiet the tingling awareness of Seth's masculinity. A need, probably adrenaline-fueled, to have wild sex with him and make the world go away.

Damn, she'd avoided that through her entire career. She knew what some of the men whispered behind her back and she didn't care. She just knew how badly getting involved with a fellow officer could mess up her career, and her career was everything to her. One little misstep and her promotion would never happen. Or she'd be accused of ugly things she never wanted to hear. The other whispers were preferable.

As for getting involved with a civilian? Well, who the hell had time? On her stateside rotations, she was usually buried in training. Either her own or that of others. Catching up, keeping up and honing her skills, not to mention getting the master's degree the air force had demanded before her promotion to major. And the war college courses. She didn't have time for much else, and joining her comrades to hang out at a bar looking for quickies didn't appeal to her at all.

She had a few good friends, people she preferred to get together with for cards or some other pastimes. No men, no sex. It kept things clean.

So why was she sitting here wondering if she'd been making a mistake all this time? Because one handsome dude had sat across from her and bought her a drink?

Damn, she needed to unwind. Her thoughts were a little messed up.

"That was some flying you did," he repeated. "I can't imagine maneuvering a bird that big into a keyhole like that and holding it steady, and you did it under some pretty heavy fire. You must have amazing nerves."

She shrugged her shoulder. "It's what I do. I've done it a lot. The reaction waits for later."

"Yeah. It does." His gaze said he knew exactly what she meant. Maybe he did. SEALs had nerves of steel, too, but maybe when they got back from a mission they needed to come down from it. *Well, hell, yeah,* she thought. She'd heard about more than one brawl involving them. Fighting out the tension probably worked as good as sex. How would she know?

Halfway through the meal, he asked something that nearly sobered her up. "You find it hard to talk to civilians now?"

"Yeah. They don't know."

His gaze grew distant. "They can't know. I don't want them to know, but even if we try to talk they haven't been here." He shook his head and came back to her. "I honestly don't want them to understand. Why should they? Bad enough we have to." He looked at his hands, fisting them then unclenching them. "But we know, don't we, Major? We know what we're capable of."

He probably more than she, she thought. Oh, heck. "Call me Edie."

"Seth," he responded. Then he shook off the mood and gave her a smile so charming it almost took her breath away. "Birds of a feather and all that. Who else can you talk to?"

"I don't know where you've been," she reminded him.

"You don't want to. I don't want to tell you, either. I just want to have some fun tonight. It was close today.

We're damn lucky you got there when you did. So I'm feeling grateful to you, grateful to be alive and grateful my team is alive. That's a lot to be happy about."

He lifted his beer in toast. "To life. Wouldn't want to be without it."

She had to laugh, and as the sound escaped her, she felt the last of her tension evaporating. She raised her own glass then sipped the whiskey.

Things seemed to become a blur after that. Later she would think she should never have had that third whiskey, even while she was eating. Or maybe she'd had a fourth?

She vaguely remembered somehow sitting at the bar with Seth as the place started emptying out. Sort of remembered him walking her back to her quarters, nothing but a tiny room, shoddily built. She remembered laughing, remembered him steadying her a bit.

Remembered him apologizing for buying her too many drinks. "I should have been able to say no." It was true. And she really wasn't that drunk.

She remembered clearly, though, waking in the wee hours. Finding him lying beside her. A quick panicked check told her she was fully clothed and so was he. They were just sleeping it off.

But as soon as the panic eased, something else surged. Wild after years of self-denial, it rose violently, like an erupting volcano: desire.

God, he was good-looking. She ran her eyes over him in the dim light from the shaded lamp across the room. Not much to see in his BDUs, but she drank him in anyway. Just once she wanted to know, and for some reason she wanted to know with this man.

Stupid, she tried to tell herself, but her body continued to grow heavy with hunger, and a deep throbbing began between her thighs. She could die tomorrow or the next day. Why did she keep putting off something so important? Because of her career?

Reasons that had made sense for a decade now all of a sudden weren't making any sense. She'd seen men and women die out here, and knew how it could come without warning, despite every sensible precaution. Life was short, and the longer she was out here the more it felt like she was riding the edge of it. How many more missions before she bought it? How many times could she cheat death?

His eyes opened and saw her looking at him. "You're a beautiful sight to wake to."

She doubted it. Living out here had made her relinquish the last female trappings. Her red hair was short, well shy of being bald the way a lot of the men went for, but short enough to be boyish. No perfume, no makeup, and messy and grungy from sleep.

But he saw something else. Flames seemed to dance in his eyes. "Me, too" was all he said.

Every last thought flew out of her head. She never thought about her own lack of protection. She didn't care that he actually pulled on a condom. She was simply past thinking.

He assumed she had done this before, and she was vaguely glad. He didn't hesitate, or question, or wonder. He just took, and that's exactly what she wanted right now.

Getting their uniforms and boots off might have been funny if they hadn't been so driven. Damn, she felt like a pillar of fire, filled with need so strong she couldn't fight it.

He tore at her clothes, she tore at his. As quickly as they could, they got naked, then tumbled onto the cot again. A narrow cot, barely making room for the two of them. Who cared?

It was fast, and it was furious. He licked and sucked at her breasts as her hands wandered naively over his back and shoulders. She didn't know exactly what to do, but her hips rose to meet his, and that seemed to be the important thing.

She'd never felt like this before. A whole new world of sensation was opening in her, and she loved it. She hadn't imagined being with a man could be so good.

Hot and heavy sensations filled her. Stifled cries escaped her. She was searching for something and didn't really know what it was.

Then he plunged into her. At once she gasped. A sharp pain seared her, almost ruining the moment.

"My God," he said.

No, don't let it stop, not now. She needed this desperately. Not knowing what else to do, she grabbed his hips and urged him on, bucking wildly in her need.

After the briefest hesitation, he bent his head again to her breast and began to move in and out of her in a steady, deepening rhythm. Carrying her higher and higher, as if she rode a rocket.

Culmination came almost too soon, as if her body had waited forever for this release. She peaked, rose up to meet him and whimpered as an almost agonizing pleasure filled her. Moments later, he drove deep into her, shuddering.

"Why didn't you tell me?" he asked later.

"I didn't want you to know."

"I'd have been more careful."

"I didn't want careful. I wanted exactly that."

He looked deep into her eyes, then nodded. "I'm leaving today. I should have told you that. Let me buy you breakfast."

She pulled on a fresh uniform, cleaned up as best she could at the sink, aware of his gaze on her.

"Don't be mad," she said finally.

"I'm not mad. I just wish I could have done better by you."

"You did just fine." She managed a smile. "I don't regret it, Seth, so don't ruin it."

At last he smiled. "Fair enough."

They went to get breakfast at the canteen. Early though the hour was, the place was filling up. With little privacy, they could only talk desultorily. He mentioned his parents, his home back in Wyoming and how he hoped to go back there soon.

She talked a little about her life back in the States, although there wasn't much to tell. No family left. That bothered her. She would have at least liked to have a family to go home to.

But mostly she talked about her career, and how it was the centerpiece of her life.

"I get it," he said. "Believe me. I'm thinking about retiring, though."

"Will they let you?"

His smile was crooked. "I'm starting to get past my use-by date. I don't see my future behind a desk."

"I hear you."

Finally he pulled a pad out of one of the many pockets on his uniform, and scribbled something. "If you need me, you can reach me through my family."

"Why would I need you?"

He just shrugged. "You never know." He rose and offered his hand. She shook it. "I hope I see you again."

She doubted he would. SEALs came and went all over the globe, almost like ghosts. Here then gone. She looked at the scrap of paper and tossed it on her plate as trash.

She didn't even dream what a mistake that might be. Or that eventually she would remember that scrawl.

Chapter One

As she approached Conard City, Edith Clapton wondered if there was even a town out here. Endless miles of empty grazing land, cattle here and there and finally a couple of roadhouses were the only signs that people actually lived out here.

Her hands tightened on the wheel, and a glance at her GPS told her she was getting close. Not for the first time she wondered if she had lost her mind.

She was pregnant. Nearly five months. And she'd spent a whole lot of time gnawing around about whether she should tell Seth Hardin he was a father. She'd tried once to track him down through the military, and had been extraordinarily relieved when she couldn't find him. She didn't want to do this, didn't want to face it, but she kept feeling she at least owed it to him to tell him he was going to have a kid.

She didn't need child support, she didn't want a stranger intimately involved in her life. Lots of good reasons for just keeping her mouth shut. Except for that feeling that a father needed to know he had a child. Whether he wanted to be part of this kid's life or not.

She couldn't seem to get around that, and God knew she had tried. Maybe the thing that had hit her hardest was the idea of having to tell this child that his father didn't even know he existed. Boy, wouldn't that make her feel like slime.

So okay, she'd drop the bomb on his parents—easier than telling him—and leave. Just leave. Get her duty done then forget about it. If Seth wanted to hunt her up someday and meet his kid, nothing would stop him. It wasn't as if she was impossible to find.

Damn, everything was all messed up. Pulled off flying status, stuck behind a desk until after her maternity leave, superior officers hinting that she might want to consider some other career path with a kid to consider. She didn't want to give up flying. She loved it. And maybe she had a hankering for the adrenaline, too.

Regardless, she was feeling an adrenaline rush as she reached town at last, and houses sprang up, most close together, most older. The time was getting close.

She wondered how she'd be received. Probably like an unwelcome messenger. Probably with anger and doubt. Well, she didn't care. She would do what was right then shake the dust from her heels.

She would try to put back together a life and a career that had been shattered by unwelcome news. Her rise to the top had probably come to a halt. How could it not, unless she gave up the baby. She couldn't do that, though. Those thoughts had danced around in her head, even pummeled her at times, but somehow she couldn't bear the idea of giving up that little life growing in her, a life that had seemed real almost from the instant she learned of it, that had become very real from the first little bubble of movement she felt.

Abandon the kid so she could continue rising? No way. She might be tied to a desk from here on out, but she'd be the best damn desk jockey in the air force, if it came to that. Maybe she had enough behind her to keep her going up, but she doubted it. Kids weren't supposed to be a factor in what assignments you could perform. You were supposed to have someone who could step in to parent while you had to be away.

She had no one. Raised by her grandmother after her mother had died of a drug overdose, she was now alone in the world. No one to turn to except herself. She was used to that. But farewell to her career, most likely. She'd make it twenty years, realize the promotions wouldn't come again, and she'd have to pull out.

Well, she wasn't going to abandon her kid the way her mother had abandoned her. That was the strongest determination in her right now.

And all of these thoughts had long since been worked out. All of them. She was just trying to avoid thinking about the uncomfortable conversation ahead. A conversation that she hoped would happen on a doorstep. Then she would turn and leave for good.

The town had slid into autumn. Leaves shone in brilliant gold. Those that had already fallen tumbled along sidewalks and streets in a light breeze. Here and there pumpkins, skeletons and waving white ghosts announced the approach of Halloween. Pretty place, she supposed, if you wanted to turn the clock back. Of course, she was a lousy judge. Sterile military environments had been her only home for a long time now.

The voice of the GPS, silenced so often in the empty prairies, resurrected and offered her no mercy. It told her to turn left, and she did, until she reached what she supposed was a newer subdivision. Post–World War II at least. Maybe post-Vietnam. Despite looking like it had tumbled out of a box that contained only one design, it was neat and even colorful. She guessed no one here thought about deed restrictions. Some of the houses were almost blinding in their brightness.

"You have arrived."

"Shut up," she said to the GPS. She slowed and stopped and looked at the house number. No escape. She was here.

The house was a white ranch-style, sprawling, set on a well-tended lawn that was beginning to fade with autumn. Rose bushes, barren of all but a few flowers, climbed a trellis beside the door. A sporty little car sat in the driveway.

She turned off the ignition and sat listening to the engine tick as it cooled. Hell, she didn't even feel this much trepidation before a dangerous mission. The neighborhood might have been empty. Not a soul in sight, not even a moving car. Unknown territory.

Well, maybe the Tates didn't live here anymore. If so, that would be the end of her search.

She realized she was thinking like a coward. Just do it. What was the worst that could happen? She got called a liar and a door slammed in her face? Hardly an incoming rocket-propelled grenade.

Sighing, she at last climbed out of the car and straightened her cammies. She refused to wear the air force's ugly pregnancy jumper, and she'd just started to show enough that she had to cover up somehow. A bigger cammie shirt, a larger waistband, they'd do for now. Later? She didn't want to think about it.

Her feet felt like lead as she walked up the path to the front door. She might be ruining someone else's life here. She didn't even know if Seth was married. Still, the sense of obligation drove her. He had a right to know, even if he wanted to forget it immediately.

And her kid had a right to know that his father had been told. If Seth wanted no part of him, she figured that would be easier to explain than not telling the kid's father at all.

Maybe.

Drawing a deep breath, she raised her hand and pressed the bell. For a minute or two there was no response, and just as she was beginning to hope no one was home, the door opened.

A pleasantly plump woman regarded her with a smile. Graying hair that still showed threads of red, bright green eyes. And damn, Edie could see Seth in her face.

"Yes?" the woman asked.

"Mrs. Tate, I'm Major Edith Clapton. I met Seth Hardin once. He's your son, right?"

"Of course he is. Would you like to come in?"

Edie shook her head quickly. "I just wanted him to know...I guess I need to tell him...well, I'm pregnant."

The woman's hand flew to her mouth. Then in an instant everything changed. Before Edie could march away as she intended, a hand clasped her arm and started drawing her inside.

"You have to come in," Mrs. Tate said. "Coffee? Tea? Maybe some milk and cookies? Oh, dear, this is...probably upsetting for you, but a pure delight to me. At least I think it is."

A delight for her? Edie felt stunned, which was probably the only reason she allowed herself to be ushered into a cheerful living room, seated on a sofa and then served cookies.

"Milk, tea, coffee?"

"Coffee if you don't mind," Edie said, almost numb with amazement. She hadn't been prepared for this kind of reception at all. "The doc says it's okay and I haven't had any yet today." Explaining something she shouldn't need to explain to this grandmotherly woman.

"Coffee is something we always have around here," the woman said wryly. "Call me Marge, please. I'll be right back."

It wasn't long before she held a mug of coffee in her hand. Those peanut butter cookies looked good, and her stomach was settling enough now that she felt she could eat one. Marge sat right beside her on the couch.

"So tell me," she said to Edie. "Everything."

Oh, God, tell this woman she'd had a one-nighter with her son at a base in Afghanistan? No way. But how could she lie? Starting with a lie would only get her in a tangle of mixed-up explanations.

Just bite the bullet.

"Seth and I met once," she said. "Over there. Just once."

"Ah." Understanding came to Marge's eyes. "I see. You haven't seen him since?"

"No. I thought about not telling him, but that didn't seem right. Anyway, if you could just let him know, I'll be on my way. I don't want anything."

"You don't want anything." Marge repeated the words. "Maybe not. You must be pretty self-sufficient to be a major wearing those wings. But what about what the rest of us want?"

Us? It was a concept Edie hadn't considered. "Seth can decide if he wants any part of this. I didn't come to pressure him. I just felt he had a right to know."

"He absolutely has a right. But then there's me. I'd

like to be part of my grandchild's life. So would Seth's father, Nate. I'm sure of that."

The complications were mounting rapidly. She hadn't bargained on a whole damn family. This was supposed to be her decision, and maybe Seth's, but not anybody else's.

"Mrs. Tate…Marge…this has to be my decision, and Seth's."

"You're not giving it up, are you?" The woman looked troubled now.

"No, I'm not giving it up. I'll raise it. But…it's my decision."

"Ultimately, yes." Marge hesitated, then shook her head. "I'm going to tell you a story. It's still painful after all these years. How well do you know Seth?"

"Not at all, embarrassingly enough."

Marge nodded. "That's all right. Things happen. I ought to know. Years ago before we married, I became pregnant by Seth's father. He went back to Vietnam and, well, my father got involved. I didn't know it, but he was stealing my letters to Nate, and stealing Nate's to me. So I thought Nate didn't want me. End result, I got shipped off to a cousin to have Seth, and he was put up for adoption."

Edie hadn't expected this. Even less had she expected her reaction to this news. She felt a twist of anguish for this woman, and for Seth, too. "I wouldn't do that."

"Times have changed. Back then, well, a girl just didn't get pregnant. It was the worst shame possible. I was young. I thought Nate had abandoned me. I was a mess and did what I was told because I couldn't see another option."

"I'm sorry."

"So was I for a long time. Then I got even sorrier. Twenty-seven years later, Seth turned up on the doorstep. I had to come clean and it nearly destroyed my marriage to Nate. It took him a while to get over the deception. So yes, you absolutely must tell Seth. I think he'd be furious if you did anything else. He has experience of those lies, you see."

Edie nodded numbly, feeling things were moving too fast, spiraling out of control. "But it's not my place to make up for your past."

Marge's face tightened. "No, it's not. All I'm asking is for you to be smarter than I was."

"I'm here." As if that answered everything. "And I need to get back." To what, she didn't know. She had a month's leave on her hands and no plans past getting this news to Seth. Marge could pass it along. "You tell him. I'm stationed at Minot right now. He can find me—us—if he wants."

She put her coffee mug on the end table and started to rise. Marge's hand on her arm stayed her.

"Please don't rush off. Nate should be here any minute, and Seth will be here for dinner. You should join us."

All of a sudden everything was mixed up. She had come here with the single-minded focus she applied to her missions. Do the job and get out. She hadn't even been sure if her self-imposed orders had been the right ones, but she had completed them. Evidently getting out wasn't going to be easy.

But how difficult could it be to appease this woman with the warm eyes, who was pleading with her to stay? Dinner? Meeting Seth's father? Seeing Seth again? Surely she had faced harder things, things she had wanted to do even less.

But she couldn't escape the fact that her mouth was growing dry and her palms damp with nameless fear, a kind of fear she hadn't felt in a long time. How could she be so afraid of seeing two people? And while Seth was a virtual stranger, she had already known him in the most intimate way possible.

So what could happen? Likely Nate would be as warm as Marge. Seth might be cold, or he might be friendly, but one way or another this would get settled and she could return to her life without any more questions hanging over her. Her duty would be well and fully completed.

"All right," she heard herself say. "Thank you."

What the hell was she getting into?

The next hour passed easily enough. Marge changed the topic to safer things, talking about her six daughters, their husbands and what seemed to be a mob of grandchildren. Edie's head was soon awhirl with names she would never sort out and was sure she wouldn't need to. Then there was some talk about how Seth's father had been the sheriff here until he retired and how glad Marge was to have him underfoot all the time. And how glad she was to have Seth home for good.

"He never blamed me for giving him up," Marge said. "Nate did, though. It was hard."

And somehow they had come back to the central reason for Edie's visit. She was actually relieved to hear the front door open. Once she got through this dinner, this meeting with Seth and his father, she could leave. She *would* leave. Six daughters? Really?

From somewhere came an irrepressible bubble of amusement, imagining the hard-edged SEAL she had met dealing with the sudden discovery of six sisters. Even if he had been a man when he met them, it must have been a culture shock.

But then she heard the door open and close, felt her heart slam with the door and looked up. Astonishment shook her to her toes as she stared at a man who resembled an older, slightly heavier version of Seth. There could be no mistaking the relationship.

"Well, hello," he said, with a smile she actually recognized.

Marge jumped up and hurried to her husband for a hug and a quick kiss. Edie clenched her hands on her lap, managing a nod and a strained smile.

"Edie, this is Seth's father, Nate. Nate, Major Edith Clapton. She knows Seth from Afghanistan. I think."

"Afghanistan," Edie said, giving a slight nod.

"So you came to visit Seth?" Nate's smile broadened and he walked into the room, extending his hand. "Nice to meet you."

Edie shook his hand, feeling the warm strength of his grip, but didn't rise. She wasn't sure her legs could hold her. A flicker of unfamiliar panic struck her. How had she let herself become roped into this?

Nate looked at his wife. "You asked the girls to come to dinner, too, I hope. I'm sure they'd like to meet Seth's friend."

Marge bit her lip. Clearly Nate was perceptive, more perceptive than most men. He looked from one woman to the other, then slowly sat in an armchair. "Okay, what's going on?"

Edie tried to frame an answer, but Marge forestalled her. "Well, dear, Seth doesn't know yet, but we're going to be grandparents again."

Nate looked dumbstruck. Edie waited tensely, alternating between the urge to just get up and walk out and the urge to shrink into the couch. All she had wanted to do was pass the word to the one person who needed to know, and now she was caught in a spiderweb of family reactions she hadn't wanted to cause, and things seemed to be growing more complicated by the second. Maybe she should have just written a letter.

But then her sterner nature returned in a surge, and she squared her shoulders. She had dealt with tougher stuff than this, countless times. At least nobody here was trying to kill her. It was ridiculous to panic. There was absolutely no reason for it.

"I should go," she said firmly. "I didn't come here intending to upset everyone. I just thought Seth had a right to know. There's no reason for either of you to be concerned about this."

"No reason?" Nate repeated the words. "Sorry, Major, but I don't agree. There's always room in this family for another grandchild. You're staying here until we're clear on that at least."

She bridled a bit and wanted to tell him that he couldn't make her stay, but she realized that wasn't what he meant. "Look," she said finally. "I only came because I felt Seth had a right to know. He can make whatever decision he wants. I don't want anything from him or anyone else."

"Really." Nate's expression hovered somewhere between a smile and a frown. "It's your decision, of course. And his."

Marge didn't look happy about the easy capitulation, but said nothing.

"Exactly," Edie said emphatically. She felt a surprising surge of warmth for the man and his understanding.

Nate settled back in his chair. "So tell me what you do in the air force, Major."

So she told him, glad of the relatively neutral topic. He asked cogent questions, indicating some military background, and he, more than Marge, seemed to understand the dangers of what she and her crew did. He didn't point them out, though, merely nodded his understanding. Marge seemed quite taken with the idea that Edie flew helicopters.

"In my day," she said, "they didn't let women do anything like that."

"They do now," Edie said.

"And in combat, too," Marge said, looking as if she hadn't really given it much thought. "My, things change."

"They certainly do," Nate agreed. "Although in my day, and probably earlier, women got right into the thick of it anyway. I saw more than a few nurses find themselves on the front lines, for all they were supposed to be noncombatants."

"At least now," Edie said, trying to lighten it a bit, "we come armed."

Nate flashed a smile.

Edie could feel her nerves stretching, despite the casual conversation. Seth was going to walk in that door soon, and she couldn't imagine his reaction. Not that she should care, she told herself. She didn't even know the man. They'd had a stupid fling, a couple of meals, then gone their own ways. Less than twelve hours.

Which made him a perfect stranger, however intimate they'd become for an hour. Therefore she shouldn't care how he reacted at all. He was a cipher in her life, a mere sperm donor. Damn, when she looked back on it, it had been so brief it really hadn't been much more personal than getting a sperm donation.

Except she knew she was fooling herself. One wild night, a night she'd never forgotten and now knew she would never be *able* to forget. Hasty, unsparing, basic lovemaking that had birthed her into a new aspect of her womanhood, and now was bringing her a totally different future. A child, a new career path.

No, she couldn't remain entirely indifferent to Seth. He'd given her two great gifts but had also ripped away all her goals and aims. Talk about a life-altering experience.

She'd been furious for a while. First at him, but she well remembered him rolling that condom on. "Even with perfect use they fail two or three percent of the time," the gynecologist had said. Great. Still, she couldn't blame Seth. She could only blame herself for giving in to impulses she had wisely avoided for years.

So she had turned the anger inward. She considered ending the pregnancy, but somehow that wasn't in her. Just wasn't something she could do, however sensible some of her friends tried to tell her it would be. Sensible ceased to matter. She sheltered a life within her womb, and when the first stirrings came, the arguments ended as far as she was concerned.

The odds had turned on her. They could have turned on her in far worse ways, and as she grew used to the idea, she began to like it. She was going to have a baby. Okay, deal. Make the best of it. And in some ways, it seemed like the best.

In others, not so much.

Like right now. She knew how angry she had been

at first. She figured Seth would feel about the same, and just hoped he didn't accuse her of fingering him as the father when it could be someone else. Hell, if he demanded a paternity test, he'd be breathing her dust faster than...

She caught herself and stopped. This was ridiculous. She didn't know how he would react and imagining scenarios wouldn't help. Just deal, the way she dealt with whatever came her way.

Marge refreshed her coffee, urging her to eat another cookie. The brief relaxation had fled, though, and the thought of trying to eat turned her stomach. This was not just a pleasant afternoon visit with an older couple. She had come to wreck some guy with news no one wanted.

She began to question all the arguments she'd had with herself about whether to tell him. Maybe she had reached exactly the wrong conclusion. Maybe she should have just left it alone.

What the hell had made her think he had a right to know? The fact that she didn't want to look into a little boy's eyes someday and admit she hadn't told his father about him?

All of a sudden that seemed very weak.

"You're doing the right thing," Nate said.

Startled by his voice, she looked at him and realized she had gone far away in her thoughts. "Why?"

"Because I know how furious I was that nobody told me. No decent man wants to find out that he was locked out of his child's life." He hitched up one corner of his mouth. "Which is not to say he might not be a little angry at first."

"I certainly was."

Nate nodded. "And I hear his car. Marge, you and I need to take a walk."

"But…" Then Marge nodded. "I guess you're right."

Nate winked at Edie. "She likes to manage things."

Marge laughed, a surprisingly girlish sound, and headed toward the door with Nate. "We'll give you a while."

Edie didn't think it was going to take long. She'd make the announcement and leave. That had been her plan all along. She should have been on the road over an hour ago.

She heard voices outside, thought she recognized Seth's deep tones. Every nerve in her body stretched tight, and even the stirring of the child in her womb didn't ease the anxiety. She rested her hand over her belly, an unconsciously protective gesture, and waited.

Seth was surprised to meet his parents on the way for a walk. As the autumn days grew more brisk, they seldom went out in the late afternoon for a stroll, but instead went earlier, before the afternoon breeze started.

"You have a friend visiting," Nate said. "We thought we'd let you talk for a while."

Then they walked off, leaving him wondering. They had seemed almost secretive, and why should he need privacy? Who the hell would be visiting him anyway? His friends were still almost all in the navy, and most were out of country right now.

Curious, he strode up to the door, wiping his hands once more on jeans that were dusty from the renovation he was doing on a house he'd bought.

When he stepped into the living room, the first thing

he registered was a camo utility uniform. Then he saw the face above them.

"Edie!" He was startled. He remembered her well, from her short red hair and bright blue eyes to the delightful curves he'd found under her baggy camos. He had been dealing with a nagging sense that he'd taken advantage of a virgin, despite what she had said, but he had never expected to see her again, even though he had hoped he might. She had seemed perfectly willing to walk away. And it had been what—five months? Surely if she'd wanted to see him again, she would have written or something. He'd given her his parents' address after all.

But there she sat, and it didn't take him long to realize she wasn't giving him a friendly smile. Far from it. He saw a tension in her face that would have been more understandable if she'd been about to leave on a mission.

"Edie?" Something was wrong. He stepped closer and hesitated. Should he shake her hand? Take a seat? Wait?

"Hi, Seth." She managed a weak smile then.

With a growing sense of dread crawling across his nerve endings, but absolutely no idea what was going on here, he decided to offer a handshake. "How are you doing?"

She shook his hand, but even as she did so that forced smile vanished.

"You look like you'd rather be anywhere else," he remarked, trying to lighten whatever was troubling her.

"I would," she said flatly.

That disturbed him even more, but he guessed whatever it was would come when she was ready. He ran a rapid mental checklist and realized there was no way she could have come bearing bad news. They hadn't known the same people. So what the hell? "Coffee?" he offered to fill the silence.

"No, thanks."

He tried a smile of his own, thinking that she was just as beautiful as he remembered. Maybe even more so. But that seemed irrelevant right now. "So what's going on?"

"I'm pregnant."

Chapter Two

Edie watched the anger rise in him, watched the fury darken his face. Then he cussed so savagely even ears accustomed to it in the military almost cringed.

"Stay here," he snapped. "Don't go anywhere."

Then he turned and stomped out. She heard the back door slam.

Stay here? Like hell. She'd done what she needed to do, and she sure wasn't taking any orders from him. Strength flooded her and she stood up. Out of here now.

But damn, he was still as handsome as she remembered. His head was no longer shaved, but sported dark hair, a little shaggy. He looked good in jeans and a work shirt. Damn, he just plain looked good.

So what? She'd delivered her message, and if his anger was any indicator, she'd never have to worry about him again.

She put her mug on the end table, straightened up and squared herself. All of a sudden she felt amazingly light. She'd finished her mission. It was over, done. She really didn't care what he thought. Having to tell him was a far cry from wanting anything from him.

And she wanted not one thing from him. Not one blasted thing. She was perfectly capable of raising a child by herself. She had done far harder things.

She walked to the front door, opened it and stepped out.

Marge and Nate Tate were right there. Apparently they hadn't gone for a very long walk at all.

"Good meeting you," Edie said brightly. "You're very nice people. Maybe I'll send you a photo when the baby is born."

"Wait," said Marge.

Edie shook her head. "I'm done here. I just came to let Seth know. He knows."

"How did he take it?" Marge asked.

"He's furious."

"He's shocked," Nate countered. "Just shocked."

"He's furious," Edie repeated. "I expected it, so I'll just go home and leave you to deal with him. Sorry I made a mess."

Nate reached out and put a hand on her shoulder. "I'm telling you, the boy is just shocked."

"SEALs don't shock easily," she said, her voice growing harder. "Please let me pass."

Nate dropped his hand and stepped to the side. Only Marge hindered her now, and the woman's gaze was pleading. "I can't stop you, but I wish you'd stay. If you won't, promise you'll at least keep in touch with us."

"I'll think about it."

Then she eased past Marge and started toward her car again. It was amazing, she thought, how good she felt to have this off her back now. Done. Finished. Now she could move on.

She had just reached her car when she heard, "Edie, wait."

She wanted to open that door, get in and peel out of here. Squealing tires would feel good right about now.

But as quickly as the light feeling had filled her, it began to seep away. Maybe she wasn't done here.

"Edie, please."

She turned slowly and faced Seth. "You don't have to say anything," she said quietly. "Not one damn thing. I can manage. I just had this conviction that I needed to let you know. I don't want anything from you, so I'm going."

"Wait," he said again, and approached slowly. "I wasn't mad at you," he said. His tone wasn't conciliatory, but firm. Not pleading. What she would have expected of a SEAL. In command, even now. "I was mad at myself. Please listen."

"There's nothing to say."

"There's plenty to say. I was mad at myself, not you. I screwed up. I didn't take good care of you."

She shrugged. "Condoms have a certain percentage of failure. Not your fault. Nobody's fault."

"But…" He hesitated. "Don't go. Not yet. I swear I won't keep you too long, but we need to talk."

"About what, Seth? That we made a mistake? That's a given. I'm actually kind of happy that it happened, now that I'm used to the idea. So I'll be fine. We're done here."

"We're not done. Not at all. I have a child on the way, too. Don't you at least owe me the consideration to discuss it?"

She realized she was starting to feel ornery and pressured, neither of which would do any good. She could either get in the car and leave, or she could stay a little longer to discuss it.

It wasn't helping that she still felt the same attraction to him that had gotten her into this mess in the first place. She tore her gaze from him and looked away, past houses to the looming purple mountains in the distance. Vaguely, she thought it was pretty here.

She supposed she owed it to him. The thought seemed to come from far away, but soon it was at the forefront of her mind. Owed it to him to discuss it. Owed it to the baby growing inside her to at least give his father a chance to be part of his life. But what did she owe herself?

That seemed to be taking a backseat. Maybe, with a child in the picture, it always would.

"Mom and Dad will leave us alone," he said. "If Mom gets too managing, we can go over to my place. But at least stay long enough to talk."

"Okay," she said reluctantly. "Just a talk."

"Just a talk," he agreed. "I need to absorb this, then we can discuss what I can do. Maybe how much of a dad I can be. I don't want you to just walk away with everything up in the air."

Everything up in the air? Just as she was feeling the situation had been settled, he was saying that? Well, she supposed it was, for him.

She shoved her keys back into her pocket and walked back toward the house beside him. Maybe the hard part was done. Maybe the conversation would be easy and civilized. And maybe they did need to talk. She had come all the way out here to give him the news for the sake of her child. Maybe this was something more she owed to the kid.

And that was a whole lot of *maybes*. She stifled a sigh. Apparently she had been wrong to think that simply delivering the news would settle everything.

Well, it might still. Nothing at all might come out of this conversation.

Marge and Nate were just inside the door. Marge beamed and announced that she would start dinner for all of them, then get a guest room ready. She buzzed away. Edie, who hadn't agreed to stay that long, felt her stomach sink.

"Don't mind her," Nate said with a faint smile. "Cooking makes her feel good. You two do what you want."

"We want a place to talk, or I can take her over to my place."

All of a sudden Marge poked her head into the room. "Seth! You can't take her to your place. It's a mess!"

Seth sighed and shook his head. "Mom, I've seen where Edie's been and I've seen what she can handle. It's far worse than my renovation mess. Before you try to start mothering, remember this—this woman flies into heavy fire to pull out people like me. She's perfectly capable of managing her own life."

Marge blinked. "Oh." Then she managed a smile. "You're right, of course. Once a mother, always a mother. I can't seem to stop."

She vanished into her kitchen again. Nate eyed his son. "Be gentle with your mother, Seth. There's a lot she can't imagine, and I'd like her to stay that way."

"I get it, Dad. But Edie extracted my team under some withering fire. I won't have her disrespected."

"It's not disrespect," Nate said. Then he turned to Edie. "Stay or go as you please. You're welcome here." Then he vanished into the kitchen after his wife.

"Wow," Edie said quietly, feeling a little warmer toward Seth after the way he had spoken for her.

"My dad was a Green Beret in Vietnam," Seth said. "I think there's a lot he's never told her."

"Wise," said Edie. She was of the school, so much

like what Seth had said, that believed there was no good reason to strip away innocence. You talked to others who had been there, or not at all.

"We can talk here in the living room, in the family room or one of the bedrooms," Seth said.

"Where's most private?"

"Anywhere, right now. Dad just went to ensure it."

She opted for the living room. She didn't want to get in any deeper, and she knew where the exit was.

She sat on the couch again, and Seth took a chair facing her. He still looked good enough to eat, she thought irrelevantly, then caught herself. This was not the time, although it helped her remember how she had gotten herself into this fix. A short period of weakness and desire had changed her whole life. And now his, evidently.

"Are you married?" she asked.

"I was." His mouth drooped a little. "Twice. Darlene bailed because she couldn't handle my lifestyle and absences. She's married to a rancher out here now. I married again a few years later. God, I loved that woman."

"What happened?"

"A drunk driver hit her when she was on her way back from parent meetings at school. I lost her."

Even as she felt a sickening pang for him, she also felt relieved. Contradictory emotions. "So I'm not wrecking a marriage."

"God, no. There's just me, and no kids. Until now." He sat back in the chair, crossing his legs loosely, and regarded her steadily. "I was a big loser on the relationship thing in my first marriage, but so far I haven't screwed up being a father. Whatever we decide, whatever *you* decide, I'm glad you told me."

"So you're not questioning you're the father?" She

was surprised to realize that the worry had been plagu-
ing her. As if it mattered, given the decisions she had
already made.

He appeared surprised. "Why would I? I may have
only met you for a few hours, but I think I got a measure
of you anyway. I picked up that honor, duty and loyalty
aren't empty words for you. I like that."

"They're not," she agreed. In fact, they were the centerpiece of her life. Everything revolved around them.
"Look, I don't see how we can discuss much. You just
found out. I needed a lot of time to work through things
myself. So maybe I should just go, give you time to think
about it, then we can talk."

She was feeling an increasing need to hit the road
again, mainly because her attraction to this man was
growing. Being alone with him once had been a major
mistake. One she didn't want to repeat.

"There'll be time," he agreed. "But first I'd like to
lay some groundwork. Areas we can discuss, what areas
you've put off-limits. And of course I need to know how
to find you. I'd hate to rattle the bars at Headquarters
Air Force, especially since they'd want to know why."

She looked away from him, trying to clear her
thoughts, to organize things. "I'm keeping the baby,
obviously."

"You thought about it, I assume."

"I did. I'm off flying status and tied to a desk. I hate
it. And I'm looking at the end of my career dreams because I'm not just going to dump the kid on somebody
else so I can racket around the world."

He remained still. Then he said, "I appreciate that."

"What?"

"That you're not dumping the kid. That you won't. I was adopted."

"Your mom told me. How do you feel about that?"

"I had good adoptive parents. I never felt a lack, until they died. Then it became paramount to track down my real parents. I can't quite explain why, but I understand it's not unusual for adopted kids to feel a real need to find their birth parents."

"I never considered it. I got a lot of pressure from friends to have an abortion. It's just not in me." Why she felt she needed to say that, she wasn't certain. Maybe because she suspected he might be wondering why she hadn't just dumped this "little problem." So many of her friends had wondered.

"I'm glad you decided against it."

"You'd never have known. And it's too soon for you to be glad about anything."

"Perhaps." He studied her as if she were a puzzle. She probably was to him. "How soon do you have to go back?"

She was tempted to lie, but she never lied. So she told him the truth, even though it might be a mistake. "I just started a month's leave."

"Then, if I can persuade you to hang around, we have time to talk and work out some things."

"What things? Just what, Seth? I can take care of this baby."

"I believe you. But have you considered the baby could have a father around, at least once in a while? If you judge me fit, anyway. I've never tried my hand at it, and as you know, my background isn't exactly preparation for fatherhood."

An odd thing happened then. It was as if a new picture overlaid an old one. Somehow Seth went from being a SEAL—rough, rugged, tough and hard to the bone—to a man who felt some uncertainty and vulnerability.

"Oh, crap," she said. She didn't want to see him that way. The other version had been safer for her.

"What?" he asked.

She couldn't answer him. She might be mistaken anyway. That was something only time would prove or disprove. "Nothing," she said. "Look, I don't want any pressure. Not for me, not for you. If you can promise me that if I stay I won't get any arm-twisting, I guess I can stay for a few days." She owed that to the baby. At least that's what she told herself.

"I can promise I won't," he said. "As for my mother, I'll do my best."

In spite of herself, Edie smiled faintly. "She was ready to adopt me."

"That's her, all right. I'll tell Dad to keep her at bay, and I'll do my best. She has a huge heart, though. It's not always easy for her to put it on a leash."

"I could see that." She liked Marge, but she didn't want the woman trying to decide her life. "I've already had enough arm-twisting. From friends, from superiors who warned me I was killing my career."

"Superior officers said that?" He looked disturbed.

"They pussyfooted around it, but the message was there. Take care of this little problem and stay on track."

"That was out of line. But I guess they wanted to see you succeed."

"Evidently. But as I've been coming to realize, there are other kinds of success. When my maternity leave is over, I'll probably move to a training position."

"Well, you have those all-important theater ribbons,"

he said. "Probably a stack of medals, too. They might keep you going. I've seen a few guys go far on a lot less, because of their connections."

"Yeah. I'm short on the connection department. And I'm not a man."

That still made a difference. She was bucking a system weighted against her and she knew it. Making full colonel was probably her limit.

She looked down and realized her hand cradled her stomach. "I've lost my waist," she remarked. "I still don't show a whole lot, though."

"You don't show at all in those cammies. Boy or girl?"

"Boy."

He smiled. "Well, I should at least know how to talk to a boy."

"You can say that with six sisters?"

He laughed. "I'm still learning."

She felt her lips twitch, and laughed, too. This hadn't turned heavy or ugly as she had feared. He was trying so hard to put her at ease, and he was succeeding. She felt herself uncoiling, relaxing, no longer poised to defend herself. Amazing.

She felt a need to change the conversation, too. The baby had been obsessing her in so many ways for so long that she needed a break. The worst was over, at least for the moment. Time for a breather. "So you're renovating a house?"

"Remodeling, really. The couple who lived there before owned it for forty years, and at some point they stopped keeping up. It's outdated, but sound."

"I take it then that you retired?"

"You bet. No desk for me."

"How's that working out?"

He laughed. "I can't seem to stay busy enough. I'm used to go-go-go. Work hard, play hard and work some more. It's a change. I could work as a deputy, but I'm not sure I'm ready for that. Or even that it's what I want. I'm kind of up in the air a bit."

She could get that. She still had her job, yet often felt that way. Somebody had picked up the jacks of her life and tossed them in the air.

Well, to be fair, she had done the tossing and she couldn't even blame a couple of drinks too many. She had been neither drunk nor hungover when she'd had sex with Seth. She'd rolled the dice and lost, with nobody to blame but herself.

Getting used to the idea that this loss might turn into a win had taken months. She certainly couldn't expect him to decide that any more quickly. But he was trying. An honorable man, if she could say little else about him yet. Honorable and respectful and sexy as hell. She wished she could remove that latter from the equation, but awareness kept insisting on tingling along her nerve endings. Damn, she could repeat her mistake.

She sighed.

"What?" he asked her.

"Just thinking."

"You look tired."

"I seem to tire more easily these days."

"Want me to see if Mom got that room ready? You could take a nap before dinner."

It was tempting, but she didn't feel ready to get that relaxed or comfortable here. "Maybe later. I do need to get my feet up, though. I spent too long in the car and I can feel my boots getting tight."

He was up and out of his chair like a shot, and pulled

a hassock over for her. She raised her feet and rested them on it. "Thanks."

"Want me to unlace your boots? To improve circulation?"

Damn, thoughtful, too. "If you do that my ankles might explode to grapefruits. Then what?"

He grinned. "You go around in your socks. No big deal." His smile faded. "I can't imagine the adjustments. I'd like to hear about them, when you feel like it."

"Sure." Dang, she was getting sleepy. It was as if the release of tension had released all her energy, as well.

"Can I get you something to drink?"

"Milk, please."

He headed for the kitchen, giving her a few blessed minutes by herself. She needed them, needed to adjust to all that had happened, most of it unexpected. Space. Just a little space.

When Seth returned, he found her asleep. He stood in the door of the living room, tall glass of milk in hand, and studied her.

She was indeed as beautiful as he remembered. The creamy skin of her face had covered her entire body, and even now his hands remembered its silken feel. She had surprisingly delicate features, too, something you didn't notice about her when she was acting, but only now, in repose. With her had returned all the memories of the night he had spent with her. She was fun, and she was hot. Very hot. One-night stands weren't his style, either, although he'd probably indulged more than he should have over the years.

But damn, he'd never expected this. Not in a million years. Conflicting feelings roiled in him. He had to do the right thing, whatever that was, but a baby? A son? Nothing had prepared him for that, and right now he felt like a fish utterly out of water, a feeling he wasn't at all used to.

There would have to be some adjustments, of course. He knew that for sure. Support. Visitation. He wasn't going to remove himself from the life of a child he had helped create. No way. But how much would Edie allow? How good would he be? Shouldn't a guy have some time to answer these questions before discovering that he had four months before the new arrival?

Well, he'd done a stupid thing, and now it had caught up with him. No input any longer about whether, now it was only how and how much. Choices had narrowed because of the reality of a new life.

He quietly returned to the kitchen to put the glass of milk in the refrigerator. "She's napping."

He should have guessed he would get cornered.

"What are you going to do?" Marge demanded.

"The right thing, Mom."

"I hope you do more than that."

Nate interrupted. "Marge, sometimes you start at the right thing because it's the only place to start."

Marge tightened her mouth. "I can't believe you got that girl pregnant."

"I'm no saint, Mom. The SEALs don't make saints."

She shook her head while her husband frowned at her. "That's not an issue anymore, Marge. Let it go."

"How can I let it go? Everything in Seth's life turned into a mess. I can understand Darlene. He warned her she wouldn't be able to take it. But Maria, too? Why do things keep going wrong?"

"She couldn't help being killed in an auto accident,"

Seth said tautly. "And frankly, I don't like being reminded of just how painful that was. Right now there's only one thing I'm concerned about."

He slid onto a bar stool beside his father and stared at his mother. "You don't know what it's like out there, and I hope you never know. But sometimes things happen. Fueled by adrenaline. Fueled by a relief that you're still alive. Edie pulled my butt out of the fire, I went to thank her, and…well, here we are. That's enough. We're here."

"We certainly are," Marge said tartly. "And you had better do the right thing because I don't want to lose a grandchild."

"And I don't want to lose a son. Maybe the only one I'll ever have. But how much of a part I'll have in his life is up to Edie. You need to understand that. This is first and foremost about Edie and the baby. I've messed her up enough already."

"We shouldn't talk about a baby as if it's a mess."

"Oh, boy," Nate said quietly beside him.

Seth felt anger start to surge. "You think not? I messed up her life. Her career. She had goals and all that's changed because she's pregnant. They're going to reassign her, maybe to training, maybe to a desk, but either way her dreams of rising high are gone now. The military might have accepted women in combat roles, but they're far from accepting the limitations on a woman who won't give up her baby or give it into someone else's care. She's refusing to do either."

"Well, of course! Giving up a baby…" Marge trailed off.

All of a sudden Seth understood what was going on here. Marge was reliving giving him up, trying to rewrite her own perceived mistake by fighting for this baby.

That was going to make this hell. Not just one woman's problems and a baby's needs, but his mother's need to correct a wrong in her own past.

He looked at his father and saw the understanding there. "Maybe I should have Edie stay at my place."

"Mebbe so," Nate said. "Mebbe so."

"She's welcome here," Marge argued.

"She's already told me she wants no pressuring and no arm-twisting. Are you going to be able to promise that, Mom?"

Marge stared at him, then suddenly sagged against the counter and closed her eyes. The kitchen was filling with the savory aroma of roasting chicken. A minute or two ticked by in silence before she spoke again. "I'm sorry, I'm not helping at all."

Nate rose and went to embrace his wife. "It's all right, honey. It's all right."

"It's okay, Mom." Seth said. "Times have changed. Edie has options you didn't, and because of that, so have I. Just let us work it out in the way that's best for both of us."

Marge nodded, her cheek against her husband's shoulder. She looked at her son. "It's just that I was so glad you came back to us. I'll never forget the joy and relief."

"And the mess." Seth gave her a crooked smile. "I messed up your life twice. So yes, a baby can be a mess until everything's sorted out."

At that Marge gave him a wan smile. "I guess so."

He rose and returned to the living room, settling in to watch Edie sleep and to think about the grenade that had been tossed his way. He needed to get used to this baby idea, and quickly. Time was wasting.

Chapter Three

Edie awoke from a dream in which her Pave Hawk was crashing into a large body of water. The sound of her name startled her, and she snapped her eyes open. Seth.

He leaned over her. "Dinner will be ready soon."

She knew one thing instantly, "I need a bathroom."

"I'll show you."

It was an urgent need, becoming more frequent as her pregnancy progressed. She had learned to go before napping or sleeping, but she'd forgotten this time. Not that she had expected to doze off on the couch.

She rose quickly. Apparently Seth sensed the strength of her need, because he led the way quickly down a hall and waved her into a small bathroom. "Take your time."

Time? What time? All of a sudden the cammies seemed cumbersome, too much material because they were too big. She struggled to get the shirt out of the way and reach the button on her pants. Damn!

When she was done, she paused before straightening her clothes and looked at her profile in the mirror, running her hands over her growing "baby bump." Smooth, not too big yet, although she was assured that was about to rapidly change. "Carrying high," one of her friends had termed it, meaning, she guessed, that she wasn't expanding outward much yet.

But her waist had certainly vanished. The changes could still catch her by surprise.

Quickly she buttoned her pants and tugged the voluminous shirt down. In the mirror she saw a woman with red hair and blue eyes, who looked tired and a little messy. Hell, she didn't even have a comb handy. Everything was out in the car.

She ran her fingers through her short hair and tried to make it lie down. A bit of water helped.

And that, she thought, looking at herself, was about all she was going to be able to do. Not inspection-ready, but looking more like she'd just finished a mission.

Oh, well.

Seth was waiting in the hall, leaning his shoulder against the wall, his arms folded. He smiled a little when he saw her. "Ready?"

"As I'll ever be."

"They don't bite, and I pretty much told Mom to lay off. I hope you like roast chicken, mashed potatoes and mixed vegetables."

"Why wouldn't I? Did you get to be picky about food?"

"Not since I joined the navy."

"Exactly."

They shared a laugh, not something she was sure she really wanted to do, but it happened. Truce time. Not that there had been a war. Yet.

Dinner was surprisingly relaxed after all that had come before. Nate regaled them with some funny stories from his years as sheriff, keeping the mood light and pressure-free.

When Edie commented on all the hand drawn and colored turkeys on the wall, Marge explained she had kept all her daughters' drawings, and put these up every year in the autumn.

"I also have their Halloween drawings, but those are in the den, if you want to see them. And then after Thanksgiving, I bring out the Christmas drawings." Marge beamed.

"Six girls make an awful lot of drawings," Nate remarked. He winked at his wife, who laughed.

"Boxes of them," she agreed. "It's a good thing we have a big attic."

"And enough wall space to put them on," Nate drawled.

Seth spoke. "But think of all the wallpapering you've escaped."

The three of them all laughed.

Edie was charmed despite herself. She had an unexpected image of keeping a trunk full of such things from her own child. This was the first time she had even dared to look that far down the road of motherhood.

Edie offered to help with dishes afterward, but Marge shooed her out, and Nate remained to help.

Once again, the offer of a room was made. She wasn't ready to accept it, though, so she left it by saying, "I'll think about it."

"I should warn you," Seth said as he followed her back to the living room, "that the only motel we have in this town would make Bagram look like the Ritz. You don't want to try to drive back tonight."

No, she didn't, but she was unwilling to commit to even a night. At least he didn't press her. Indeed, he seemed to be working very hard not to press her in any way.

Something to be grateful for. In fact, maybe there was a whole lot to be grateful for.

She settled again on the sofa and put her feet up. "Are you sure you don't want to take those boots off?" he asked.

She just knew that if she took them off she wouldn't get them back on tonight. The question was whether she wanted to risk walking out of here barefoot. The answer was no. Experience had taught her to keep her boots on unless she was safely at home.

He sat facing her again, this time with his elbows on his splayed knees. Relaxed, yet not. For a moment she wished she could just close her eyes and fall back to sleep. Dinner had given her a sense of contentment that was rapidly vanishing. Tension steadily crept into the air.

"Tell me about it," he said quietly. "How you found out, how you felt."

"That's huge."

"Take your time. I'd like to know."

She hesitated, then said bluntly, "I think I knew at some level right away."

"Really?"

"Well, I always used to finish off a mission with a meal and a couple of drinks. I never drank again after that night. I told myself it was because I needed to stay out of any more trouble."

"That would make sense." He stirred a little, but his gaze never wavered. "I also suspect you guessed. I've heard my sisters say they knew almost to the moment, before they were even sure."

"Well, maybe something happens fast. I don't know. I just lost all desire to wind down with a drink." She shrugged her shoulder. "Whatever. When I missed my period, I thought it was stress. But I knew, Seth. Somehow I knew. I did a great job of denial."

"I can imagine."

He probably could. Only she hadn't given him the opportunity to do that. He waited, and finally she decided to tell him more.

"When I missed my second period, I felt like I'd been hit over the head. I couldn't deny it anymore. I wanted to ignore it, but...well, even as I was getting mad, and having wild urges to run away from reality, I couldn't ignore it. Even when I couldn't stand the thought I felt like I had to do what was right for the kid. That meant seeing the doc."

She closed her eyes briefly. "I can't explain. I was seriously mixed up for a while, bouncing between fury and despair. I was taking prenatal vitamins and trying to tell myself it wasn't true. I look back at it and hate myself."

"Why?"

"Because that's not me. I don't run from things. I deal with them."

"Blame it on shock."

"Yeah." She gave an unsteady laugh. "I was still in shock when they grounded me and sent me home. I could have still done the job, you know."

"I'm sure you could have."

Again her hand came to rest on her swelling belly. "What's best for the kid. That stress wouldn't have been good."

"It really shook up your life."

"Top to bottom." No point in denying it. "Everything changed, and it changed fast. Well, except for the emotional roller coaster. And the morning sickness. It took a while for that to pass."

"Was it bad?"

"Awful, for a while. And you might as well paint it

on a billboard when you show up for duty every morning with soda crackers."

At that he smiled faintly. "Oops."

"Yeah." She shook the tension from her shoulders. "I needed a while to face it all. I kept looking for ways to get around it. Ways I could manage my career and a kid. The two aren't going to mesh well."

She looked beyond him, into the past, knowing she was minimizing the turmoil she'd endured as she adjusted. "I felt betrayed," she admitted. "Not by you, but by my body. God, how many women get pregnant from one time, when a condom is being used? The doc wasn't sympathetic to that argument. He just said flatly, 'It happens. Condoms aren't failure-proof.' He said next time I should be on the pill." She shook her head. "Next time? There wasn't even supposed to be a first time."

"I'm sorry."

"No. Don't even go there. I'm a grown woman. I did something I knew damn well I shouldn't have. That I'd never done before because I didn't want to submarine my career. I know it caused some talk about me that I didn't ever go with a man, but I didn't care. It was better than what they'd say if I dated the wrong man. Besides, I didn't want any messes."

"And I handed you one of the biggest of all." He looked annoyed again.

"Hey, it took two of us, and I don't remember protesting."

One corner of his mouth lifted. "At least let me own my share of the blame. It *did* take the two of us."

She didn't say anything, but looked down at her hands resting on her tummy. He drew her too strongly. Getting away from him might be the only smart thing she could do now. But the baby...

She sighed. "But back to the saga. I argued for a while that I could do my job. I believed it, too. Except they were right and after they grounded me, even I could get it. I'd be up there with something to consider besides my job. I could put a lot of people at risk worrying about the baby. And, frankly, I don't think I was emotionally stable. Not then, maybe not now."

"What do you mean?"

"I woke up every morning hoping I'd find out I'd been dreaming. Wishing doesn't make it so. Plus, I started taking things harder. Closer to tears. Closer to anger. My judgment was affected by my emotions. It's good they grounded me." He looked so damn sympathetic that she glanced away. "Regardless, after a lot of arguing with myself, I started planning a different future. Then it occurred to me that it wasn't right not to tell you."

"That must have thrilled you."

"Not exactly. But in the end it all comes down to one thing, and it will from here on out—what is best for this baby. It's a major adjustment. I don't expect you to make it quickly or easily. You don't even have to make it at all. But once I got my priorities straight, stressful as it was, things got clearer. Not easier, but clearer."

He nodded. "I can see that."

She fell silent, looking down at her hands clasped over her belly. "I've had a lot of time to work this through. You deserve some time, too. I should leave and give you space."

"Quit trying to hightail it, Edie. My role in all that's coming is better decided by the two of us together. You can walk out and take it all on your shoulders, but what decisions can I make without talking to you? Not very many. I'm not going to pretend it wasn't a shock. It was. But now I have to deal with it, too."

When she didn't speak, he continued.

"We may not have gotten here in the most responsible, thoughtful, well-considered way, but that doesn't matter anymore. What matters is what we do now. And that's something that has to be discussed. From now on, we're linked by a life we created. How we handle that link is everything."

"I've thought about that," she replied quietly.

"I'm sure you have. Now I have to think about it. I'm sure you've considered how to reshape your life, and I'm equally certain that picture didn't have me in it. Well, now I'm in it, and I'm not walking out of it."

Everything had grown more complicated. But had she honestly believed she was going to walk out of here with nothing changed? Had she truthfully believed that he'd offer child support or something and then dismiss her? Forget about it?

But she didn't really know Seth Hardin, and that was a big problem. She knew next to nothing about the kind of person he was out of uniform and she needed to know that before she made any decisions about how little or how much he could have to do with her child. Their child.

God, how stupid could she be? Just come out and make the announcement because it was the right thing to do? Then go back like nothing had happened? Had she really convinced herself of that?

Or had something else been going on?

Damned if she knew. Damn.

"I don't know you," she said.

"I don't really know you, either. That's our first hurdle. We can't really decide anything until we get to know each other a little better. Yes, you could go back to duty and I could just write a check once a month, but I won't be satisfied with that. Not unless I'm convinced there's no other way."

It shook her a bit to realize that she'd been expecting exactly that—that he'd want no part of this, other than to write an obligatory check, which she didn't even want, and she'd get the hell out of this intact with no messy entanglement. That she'd already be on the road with a clear conscience. She had intended to do the right thing, but she hadn't expected him to do more than the minimum.

What guy wanted a kid this way? None, she had thought. Evidently she had been mistaken. At least about this man.

Messier and messier. She put a hand up and tried to rub the growing tension from her neck.

"This is too intense," he said. "Too much too fast. You're exhausted and you must feel like I'm pushing you. How about I show you a guest room. I can set you up with a TV for distraction, or a book, and you can get those damn boots off and relax. We have some time. I don't want to wear you out."

It sounded so good, to just have some space and time. She was feeling pushed and overwhelmed, all right. But the thought of staying here, of dealing with Marge, who clearly had her own hopes about this, was daunting. It wasn't that she didn't like Marge, it was that she didn't want her arm twisted, however subtly, and she was certain the woman would find a way.

She was acting like a coward, a whole new view of

herself, but she honestly just didn't want to handle any more. She'd been handling enough of this major life upheaval and needed a break.

"I'll go to the motel."

"Like hell." He hesitated. "All right, if you don't think you can deal with my family, you can stay at my place. It's livable. I'll just come back here for the night. You'll rest better if you're not right on the highway directly across from a truck stop."

It struck her that she was not only being cowardly, but she was also unreasonably discommoding Seth. He probably preferred his own bed in his own house, however torn up it might be. Either way, she wasn't going to be perfectly comfortable in strange surroundings, so she might as well minimize the inconvenience.

"No," she said finally. "I'll just stay here. But I'm exhausted."

"You look it. Come on."

He took her to a girlish-looking room that smelled fresh, and the covers on the bed were even turned down. "Water?" he asked.

"Please."

"Do you get the nibbles at night?"

She flushed faintly. "Sometimes now."

He smiled. "Eating for two."

"Not quite. But sort of."

A chuckle escaped him. "Anything you can't eat?"

She shook her head. "I've been warned away from shellfish, but nothing else."

"Good enough."

She was sitting on the edge of the bed working her boots loose when he returned with a tall glass of ice water and a small plate of cookies. "This okay?"

"That's wonderful."

He set them on the night table, then squatted. "Let me help with those things. Did you bring a bag?"

"Hell, yeah. I forgot. It's in the car."

"I'll get it." He worked the laces swiftly and tugged the boots off. "Let the dogs breathe," he joked. "Be right back."

She piled the pillows and leaned back, stretching her legs out, feeling almost instant relief. A few minutes later Seth was back with her duffel and placed it on a chair. "No one will bother you. The hall bath is all yours. Mom and Dad have their own. Just make yourself comfortable."

"I already am," she admitted.

He paused by the bed, touching her cheek lightly with his fingertips. "You're a beautiful, brave woman, Edie. Thanks for keeping me in the loop. See you tomorrow."

Then he slipped out.

She wanted to wash up, brush her teeth, get into something more comfortable. But she felt as if her whole body had turned to lead. Contenting herself with unbuttoning her pants, she reached for the light switch and turned it off.

Sleep claimed her almost before she dropped her arm to the mattress.

Seth went out to bid his parents good-night. "She's asleep," he said. "Just let her be. The woman is worn out."

"Of course we'll let her be," Marge said. "Why would you think otherwise?"

"In the morning, too," Seth said. "Please."

Marge pursed her lips. "All I had in mind was pancakes."

"Sure."

Nate laughed. "I'll keep an eye on it. But you know your mother is a good woman."

"Of course she is. It's just that I get the feeling Edie has been pushed too much. If you can believe it, her superior officers hinted around for her to get rid of the baby."

Marge gasped and a frown lowered over Nate's brow. "Just a little out of line, wouldn't you say?"

"Completely out of line," Seth said, agreeing with his father. "But that ought to give you some idea of what she's dealing with along with having her career plans wrecked and her whole life turned on end. What she needs is space. I intend to give it to her."

"But," Marge said quietly, "you two have things to work out."

"And we will. But not in a pressure cooker. Right now, as stupid as it sounds to say about a woman like her, I want her wrapped in cotton wool."

At that Marge smiled. "That's a good idea. Cotton wool it is."

"Thanks, Mom."

"Stay a few," Nate said. "We're having our bedtime coffee. You can't possibly turn that down."

Unlike many folks who claimed they couldn't drink coffee at night, the Tates always did. That last cup seemed important, and when he was here he often joined them.

"There's one question that hasn't been asked," Nate said when Seth returned with his own mug to the table. "How are *you* feeling about all this?"

"Stunned," he said frankly. "But it's wearing off. Now I'm trying to think of ways to take care of this. The last thing I want to do is diminish Edie in any way, but I'm not going to pretend I don't have a son."

Nate spoke then. "You admire that woman, don't you?"

"If you'd seen her hauling us out, you would, too. She took risks she could have refused to take. Her rotors couldn't have missed the rocks by more than a few inches. She's strong, she's brave and she's determined. And she's a damned fine pilot."

"So she flies helicopters?" Marge asked. "What kind?"

"A Pave Hawk, a modified Black Hawk. She comes in to extract downed pilots, units that are in trouble, that kind of thing."

"She gets shot at."

"Yes, Mom, she gets shot at."

Marge cradled her mug in both her hands and fell silent for a little while. Then she said, "I guess she wouldn't appreciate mothering."

"Pilots do have a bit of ego," Seth said in an attempt at humor.

Marge answered tartly. "You mean like SEALs?"

Seth laughed. "Well, not quite as bad."

Marge flashed a smile. "I just want to understand something, Seth. Why didn't you have any children with Darlene? I mean, I know it couldn't have happened with Maria, she died so soon, but Darlene made it almost two years."

He tensed, feeling a whole lot of stuff flood back that he'd tried to bury. "Because I never knew if I'd be around to see a kid grow up. I was gone a lot, and couldn't even guarantee to ever come home."

"Nobody can be sure of that."

"But not everyone opts to go to the places I went. Or take the risks I took. That was part of it, anyway."

"And the rest?"

"We weren't married long enough to be settled with each other. I wasn't the only one with qualms because I wasn't home much. Can we let that go? Everything's different now."

It surely was, he thought as he climbed into his car and headed back to his house. Very different. He was retired, and still adjusting to having to make his own plans for each day, still adjusting to a quieter, slower pace. But he'd be around. At least for a while.

The question was whether Edie would be around.

For the first time, he stopped focusing on Edie and the immediacy of the news and started thinking about what this could really mean to him.

He wasn't at all sure about any of it.

Chapter Four

Edie awoke in the morning feeling well rested and with a surprisingly positive thought: if she'd made the biggest mistake of her career, at least she hadn't made it with a total jerk.

Seth might still turn out to be one, but so far he hadn't been. A little pushy about being part of her kid's life, but that was excusable. For the rest, he was acting far better than she had expected.

She stretched, grabbed some fresh cammies from her bag and her travel kit and headed for the bathroom. A long, hot shower sounded good. She felt absolutely cruddy from the lengthy drive yesterday, and while her career had taught her to get used to it when necessary, it wasn't necessary now.

As she stepped into the hallway, she smelled the delicious aroma of frying bacon, and her stomach rumbled. Being hungry more often was something she was still getting used to, just like she was still getting used to needing the bathroom more frequently, and the changes in her body. Hell, the changes in her emotions, come to that. She had always thought of herself as being on a pretty steady keel, but the baby had been changing that. Until the past few months she never would have dreamed of bursting into tears over something a superior said to her.

Lots of changes and more to come.

Like maternity clothes. So far she had avoided buying them. Cammies passed on base and at work. But if she wanted to go anywhere else, they wouldn't do.

She almost sighed. She guessed she was still trying to avoid some basic realities here.

She put her things away, picked up the plate and glass from last night and made her way to the kitchen with some uneasiness. She really didn't trust Seth's assurance that his mother wouldn't pressure her. She was getting sick of pressure to do things she didn't want to do. It was entirely different from the pressures of the career she had chosen. This was personal.

But Marge took her dishes with a warm smile and told her to take a seat. "I made blueberry syrup this morning. I'd better warn you it's not very sweet, but Nate and I have to watch our waistlines."

"I love blueberries."

"Good. Pancakes and bacon."

Edie slid onto a stool, even though in some other part of the house she could hear Nate and Seth talking. Amazing, she thought, how things had slowed down. Yesterday she had planned to come and go like a whirlwind. Now here she was waiting for breakfast and what would come next.

As she watched Marge buzz around, she thought about Seth some more. She had liked him from the outset, but she liked him better now. As near as she could tell, he was being utterly honest with her. Could she ask for more than that?

And attractive. Damn, she wished that would go

away. Finding him desirable could only muddy this mess more. Who needed that? Nor was it likely that he felt the same pull toward her. She remembered how he had looked at her just before they had made love, and that expression wasn't there now.

No, he was handling her with kid gloves. Hardly surprising. She supposed she had lobbed a grenade at him. He'd have been justified in telling her to get lost. Instead he wanted to be part of this baby's life. God, that was only going to make things messier.

As she tried to imagine how they could manage that, what with her career, she felt a kind of despair seeping into the morning. This couldn't work. Absolutely could not. They had different lives. How could anyone pull that together?

She had believed she had faced all the complications already, but they just seemed to be growing.

All from one stupid mistake in the middle of a war zone. All from creating one life purely by accident. She was glad of the baby now in so many ways, even as she struggled with all the changes it would mean. Now she had thrown Seth into the equation. Rightfully, he would want some things.

Could she give them?

The realization struck her that she didn't even understand the kind of life these people were living, not anymore. It had been too long, too many years of being in service, with all that entailed. She hadn't been part of anything approaching a real family since her grandmother had died. She didn't understand how they worked. Didn't understand how to make one. Maybe just leaving would be the best thing.

But the baby stopped her. Maybe she didn't know

how to do it, but these people obviously did. Maybe she could learn something, a different way of living and thinking. For the sake of the baby, she should probably give it a shot.

They ate breakfast at the dining table in the kitchen. Seth told a few jokes. Marge reminisced a little about her daughters. Nate had a few more stories about being sheriff. All safe, all comfortable. Edie even managed to summon a few amusing stories of her own, although when she thought about it, she began to wonder if she hadn't been too damn serious for too damn long. The few things that occurred to her didn't seem fit for mixed company.

Black humor went with the job, and while Seth and Nate might get it, she seriously doubted Marge would. She looked at Seth's mother, feeling a little amazed at how protected the woman seemed to be. Yet maybe there were ways she hadn't been protected at all. Just from what she had said yesterday, there had certainly been sorrows and worries in her life.

The common fate of humanity, it seemed.

After breakfast, Seth suggested they go over to his place. "You might as well see what I'm up to these days."

Renovating a house sounded like an alien world to her. She was only too happy to go with him, to escape the family setting to something much less daunting. To get away from a situation that was making her feel her lacking as a person.

Seth's house wasn't that far away, but definitely in an older part of town. Two stories with dormers, it clearly needed a coat of exterior paint, but otherwise it looked fine.

"Why did you get a house?" she asked.

"Something to do. And since I'm probably going to be staying around here...well, I'm a little too old to move in with my parents, don't you think?"

The wry question almost made her laugh. "You seem to be very close to them."

He pulled into the short driveway, which faced a detached garage. "I am now." He switched the SUV into Park but didn't immediately turn off the engine. "I think," he said, "I can identify a little with how you felt coming here yesterday."

"You can?"

"I showed up unannounced to tell Marge I was her long lost son. I sweated it a bit."

"I know I would."

"The funny thing was, I didn't even have to say it. She took one look at me and knew. She said I looked exactly like my dad."

"You look a lot like him," Edie agreed. "But I can see your mother in you, too."

"Before you go, she'll probably pull out some pictures of him and me at the same age. She gets a kick out of the resemblance."

Edie hesitated. "I gather it caused a storm, though."

"Big-time." He drummed his fingers on the steering wheel. "Dad was furious that she'd never told him, that she'd kept me a secret for all those years. He moved out for a while. I felt like hell for causing that."

"But they worked it out."

"Obviously. Dad mentioned once that he'd had to do some serious thinking about the kind of husband he was, too. They've been closer ever since. And now I've got a whopping big family with sisters, their husbands, nieces and nephews. A couple of the girls still live in town. Maybe you'll meet them."

"Maybe." She wasn't committing to a single thing yet.

"Do you have any family?"

"No." She realized her answer sounded too abrupt, and really, she didn't want to be difficult, at least not yet. That might come later. "My mother overdosed when I was little and I was raised by my grandmother. There was nobody else."

"So you never knew your father?"

"No." Now she felt as if she'd been stripped naked. He'd probably assume she had come looking for him because she had never known her own father. Well, maybe that was part of it, but only a small part. "In my case, nobody knew who the father was."

"Ouch." He drummed his fingers again, thinking, then dropped it. "Let's go inside. You can tell me how awful my color choices are."

"As if I would know."

She was grateful he had let it go and was willing to lighten the moment. Dealing with the child they had created, deciding how to handle the kid's future, did *not* mean she had to expose her entire life to him.

He didn't insist on helping her out of his car, for which she was grateful. Those courtesies were a thing of the past, if they'd ever existed in her life. She was an officer, an equal, and she expected to be treated that way. Gender didn't enter into it.

The porch creaked a little under their feet and when he unlocked the front door, it squealed a bit. "I keep meaning to oil those hinges."

"Well, you'll hear anyone come in."

He laughed. "Around here that's not as big a deal as some places we've been."

She looked around, surprised by the tidiness. She had been expecting much worse. The mere idea of remodeling a house had led her to expect total chaos and dust. Instead she saw spacious rooms with beautiful wood floors, lots of sunlight and some freshly painted walls.

"I told you it wasn't too bad. I was thrilled when I stripped away old carpet and linoleum and found oak floors. But I've been working one room at a time, mostly, to keep it under control. First the living room, then my bedroom and my bath."

"You've done a lot in a short time."

"I started last year when I was on leave, but I haven't had much else to do with my days since I retired. Mostly the place needed to be freshened up, but the bathrooms needed redoing, and my next project is the kitchen. It's a big room but could be a lot more useful."

They climbed the stairs together. "That bathroom is going to blow you away," he said.

"Why?"

"Because I went overboard. I don't have to tell you how important a really good shower can be. I know about conservation and all that, but this I couldn't resist."

Neither could she when she saw it. Her eyes widened with delight. A walk-in shower with several nozzles and even a bench to sit on. Everything gleamed with brand-new beige tiles and brand-new fixtures.

"Wow! I could live in that shower!"

He laughed. "So could I. I try not to overdo it, but sometimes I could just sit there with the hot spray beating forever. I always felt a good shower was a great luxury. So it's my luxury."

"I can't think of a better one. It looks like something out of a magazine."

"I think that's where I stole the idea from."

She laughed. "Good steal."

"The bedrooms are pretty much just bedrooms, but they have nice big closets. And I put in insulated windows over the summer. That was some job. I'm learning as I go."

Downstairs he showed her the kitchen. It was indeed large, and very much underutilized. "Maybe you'll have some ideas about what I should do with it."

"Me? I haven't cooked since I put on my uniform for the first time."

He cocked a brow at her. "Mess hall, huh? Me, too, mostly. But I gotta have a kitchen. It's not like this town is loaded with restaurants. I can't keep eating with my family or going to Maude's diner. She'll turn me into a blimp."

"So you're going to learn to cook, too?"

"Absolutely. I expect I'll get some lessons, too, whether I want them or not. But I still have to figure out the best way to organize this room. And since I don't cook I haven't the foggiest idea."

"Steal another magazine idea."

He laughed. "Sure. It might look nice, but what if it doesn't function well?"

He had a point. She had to smile. "Are you feeling like a fish out of water?"

"In more ways than one. It'll come to me eventually."

"So what's your plan for remodeling today?"

"I wing it. I was thinking about tearing out some drywall in the back bedroom. From the look of it, it got wet. The roof must have leaked at one time or another.

But I don't want to do that while you're here. It'll make dust and I'm not sure that's safe."

"I could be somewhere else."

"Not if I have anything to say about it." He pulled two chairs over to a minuscule dinette. "How about some lemonade? I practically live on the stuff."

She sat gingerly, unsure of the chair, but it seemed safe. He brought her a glass of lemonade, then leaned against the chipped counter as he held his own. "How about you?" he asked.

"What about me?"

"Anything you'd like to do today? See the sights? See the town, such as it is?"

She hesitated. "Why would I want to see the sights?"

"Because they're there?" He grinned. "More time to get to know each other, too. Without pressure, I promise."

She could hardly argue with that. She looked down at her cammies, though. "Any place I can buy something else to wear first? I'm tired of walking around in a tent, but so far I've refused to buy any maternity clothes. I'd love a pair of jeans again."

"We're a small town but we've got Freitag's. It may not have the biggest selection in the world, but it's got a little of everything. Unless you're looking for high fashion, they must have something."

After they finished the lemonade, he drove her over to the department store. It reminded her of such stores when she was little in a small town. Not the big modern boxy places, but the kind of store where everything was crammed in and old wooden floors creaked beneath every step.

She did have some different jeans to choose from, and

a few tops that didn't strike her as too frilly or cutesy, but basically the kind of gear even a pregnant woman could work in if she needed to.

When she had made a few selections, she came out of the dressing rooms in jeans with an expanding panel and an extra-long shirt that resembled a man's button-down. Good enough. The cammies were in her bags.

Seth had waited for her at the front of the store, giving her the time to make her own choices. She appreciated that he hadn't tried to be part of it. She'd been buying her own clothes for a long time.

"That looks more comfortable." He smiled. "I mean, cammies are okay, but an awful lot like wearing a tent, even when they fit. Have you got a jacket? It's getting chillier here."

So she added a jacket at the last minute, something she figured would do for a few days. When she got back to Minot, she was going to have to shop for a brutal winter, but she didn't need to do it yet. Not for here.

Outside, they paused beside the car after he tossed her bags in the backseat. "The question," he said, "is what you'd like to see. I could take you up into the mountains to see the old mining town. It's picturesque, but it can't be explored because the old tunnels are collapsing." Then he faced her. "Or would being in the mountains bring back memories you don't want?"

That was a thoughtful question. She half smiled. "I mostly saw them from above."

"True. So the mining camp? I should stop at the diner and get us a picnic lunch. In case we get hungry."

Some part of her wanted to take over and make some of the decisions, not just become a passenger on this tour. Yet, she reminded herself, he *was* asking her. He had given her every opportunity to say no, or change the plans. Including agreeing when she said she wanted to get some clothes.

Maybe he was being too amenable, she thought as she waited in the vehicle while he ran into the City Diner. And maybe she was just making up reasons to be irritated. None of this was turning out as she had anticipated. She ought to know by now how little of life actually followed the plan.

The thought eased the niggling irritation she had begun to feel for no good reason. One of the things about her pregnancy that still surprised her was the rapidity with which her moods could change. She'd never been a moody person, but now she could sometimes swing as fast as a pendulum. She had to keep catching herself, and she was rapidly discovering that when she felt something, her mind quickly tried to serve up a reason for it.

It had been easier at work, though. Much easier. There the sheer predictability and patterns had made it possible to remain fairly stable. Now she was out of her element, and it was exposing things in herself she hadn't faced before.

On the way out of town, Seth said, "If you need to stop for any reason, let me know. I'm not exactly a vet at pregnancy, but I can remember my sisters talking about things like not being in the car for too long. As for bathroom facilities, we'll have to rough it out there."

Oh, great, she thought. "Do you know how hard that is for a woman?"

He slowed down. "Then maybe we shouldn't go so far."

"Is there any place to go around here that isn't far?" She managed to sound wry.

He laughed. "No, actually. Your call."

The words acted like a balm. "Hell, let's go for it. I can always find a tree." It wasn't as if she hadn't faced these things before. Survival training had taught her a lot.

As they headed toward the looming mountains that looked so different in the morning light than they had yesterday afternoon, she had an uncustomary fanciful thought that it was almost as if they had personalities. Moods. Like her.

She prided herself on being hardheaded and practical. Thinking mountains had personalities and moods lay far off the beaten path for her. More changes?

"Tell me about yourself," she said to Seth, desperate to keep from wandering into crazy places. A dangerous question since she wasn't sure how well she wanted to know him. The physical attraction she felt was already dangerous enough.

"Where do you want me to start? We pretty much covered that I was adopted, and didn't find my birth parents until later. I've got a big family now, but you know that. Or are you looking for career details?"

"I don't know," she admitted. "There's the outline and then there's other stuff."

"Yeah, the other stuff. The hard stuff to talk about." He shook his head a little. The car bumped slightly in a small rut as they started to climb. Her hand flew to her belly.

"You okay?" he asked.

"Fine. Holding my stomach seems to be turning into an unconscious habit."

"It did with my sisters. One used to make fun of

how she could set a cup of coffee on what she called her shelf."

Edie smiled. "I haven't gotten there yet."

"Clearly. Okay, about me. Well, I don't know that I'm the most interesting guy in the world. I did a job and I can't talk about any of it. That's really helpful. Just over twenty years in the SEALs and it's almost all redacted in heavy black ink."

Now she laughed. "That's true for a lot of my background, too. How much trouble are you having returning to civilian life?"

"Not as much as I expected. Maybe more than I hoped. When you're regimented most of the time, it's weird to have to get up every day and figure out what you're going to do with it. There's something else, too."

"What?"

"I had a strong sense of purpose before. It's gone now, and I miss it. But maybe that's changing."

She stiffened a little. "Don't make me or this baby your mission."

Now his voice hardened. "You can't stop me from making my son my mission. Let's be clear on that right now. You may be able to set limits, but you can't walk away with my son as if I never existed."

Anger seethed in her. "Are you threatening me? Take me back right now!"

"Why? So you can do the combat search and rescue thing? Fast in, fast out?"

"Damn you, Seth Hardin!"

He pulled the car off the road under some tall pines, jammed it into Park and swiveled to face her. She saw then the SEAL, the man who went into impossible situations, did impossibly difficult things and never backed down. He could have been carved from steel.

"This is my child, too," he said sternly. "The sooner you get really used to that idea, the sooner we can work things out amicably. But you are not, I repeat not, going to carry on as if that child isn't mine, too."

"I don't need you!"

"But that child does. That boy is entitled to whatever I can give him. Because I helped make him, Edie! Like it or not, I am his father."

"You didn't want this baby!"

"Neither did you. And while it's all good and well for you to come out here and tell me about it because you felt a duty, it remains I have a duty and I'm not going to shirk it. Period. All that talk about how you can handle it on your own? It was nice, I believe you could, but as long as I'm breathing, you're not going to have to and that boy isn't going to be fatherless. That's my bottom line. Deal with it."

She glared at him. How dare he? It was her body, her child, her life, and he had no right, absolutely no right, to come in and make demands on her or give her orders. Or threaten her.

Seth faced forward but he didn't put the car in Drive. He drummed his fingers on the steering wheel, and blew a long breath between his lips. "I shouldn't have blown up. There's something you need to understand about me. When I'm attacked or threatened, I'm trained to go on the attack. I guess I need to work on that."

"Threatened? How did I threaten or attack you?"

He turned to look at her and his eyes were almost haunted. "You keep talking about leaving. How you're capable of handling this by yourself. How you don't need or want anything from me. You're threatening the possibility of not allowing me to be part of my child's life every time you do that."

She caught her breath. What the hell? Then it hit her like a ton of bricks. He'd had a wife leave him because she couldn't take life as a SEAL wife. How many scars must that have left? And every time she said she wanted to leave, he must be hearing echoes of that.

Every time she said she could handle this on her own, every time she said she didn't want anything from him, every time she suggested just going back to work…God, he must have heard a version of all this before, when his first marriage ended. She was just trying to be reasonable and take responsibility for her own life, but he must be hearing a string of rejections: *I don't want you. I don't need you.*

She looked down at her tightly clenched hands, resting, as usual, now right over the baby. Her attempts to be responsible and independent made perfect sense—until she turned it around and looked at it from his perspective. How many times could you tell a man you didn't need him, even as a father to his own child?

Not many. She averted her face and looked out the window into the shadows beneath the pines. Almost without realizing it, she began to speak quietly.

"I've been spending a lot of time looking at my life in a shattered mirror."

"Shattered mirror?" he prompted quietly.

"You know how it looks? Fragmented, jumbled, not recognizable. I've been fighting to put those pieces together in some way that produces a recognizable image. It hasn't worked very well in some ways. In fact, I'm getting a whole different image, but it's still broken up a bit."

"I guess so."

"Anyway, I'd worked out as much as I could on my own, and like I always do, I took the bit between my teeth. I was going to do it, and was going to do it *my* way." She sighed and looked at him. "I wasn't really thinking, I guess. At least not about you."

Something in his face softened a bit. "Why should you have thought about me? You don't know me. You didn't know how I'd react. Maybe I wouldn't want any part of this. You couldn't know. But I do want a part of this, and we need to start from there. So if you'll quit making me feel like the thing you want most is for me to turn my back on this baby, I'll hang on to my temper and be as reasonable as I can."

He put the car in Drive and pulled back onto the road. "The mountain aspens are starting to be threatened by climate change. We're losing a lot of them. But I know a place where they look beautiful right now. Why don't we check that out before we go to the mining town? Okay?"

"Sounds good to me." Looking at trees sounded peaceful, and right then she wanted some peace. She had some new things to consider, mainly what she had learned and realized about Seth. Somewhere in her mind, she had clearly been fitting him into a stereotype of some kind.

A man who naturally wouldn't want a kid, especially with a woman he wasn't married to. Yeah, that was one stereotype she'd been applying. She'd come out here because of a sense of duty to the child, and she'd been almost convinced that he'd shrug it off, maybe demand she prove it was his, maybe offer a token monthly check.

Well, he had certainly shattered that stereotype. One which probably wouldn't be accurate about a lot of men if she were to be fair. How would she know? She knew men at work and men in battle, and very little else about them. She knew some of them had kids they loved but they were married. Certainly she had never met anyone who'd fathered a child in a one-night stand. At least no one who admitted to it.

But Seth was a unique case any way she looked at him. Given up for adoption. Now back with his birth family. He probably had more reasons than most to want to be a part of this child's life.

She couldn't have known any of that before coming here, but she knew it now, and she needed to take it into consideration, along with the wounds from his first wife leaving him.

"I wonder," she said, "how much of all that determination to do this myself had to do with my parents."

"I think you're just naturally a doer and a problem solver. Look what you do for a living, after all. But what exactly do you mean about your parents?"

"I told you I never knew who my father was and that my mother died of an overdose. Maybe I'm just determined to ensure that doesn't happen to this baby."

"I wouldn't be surprised," he agreed. "We're the sum of our experiences, all of us. Whatever is behind it, I'm damn glad you made the choice you did. Even if I didn't look like it yesterday. Seriously, Edie, I was mad at myself, not you. I didn't advance in the SEALs because I was careless of other people, and my first reaction was that I'd been stupid and made your life hell and that at my age I should know better."

"We both should have known better." She sighed, then smiled faintly. "But I still don't regret it."

He laughed then, and the very air seemed to lighten. "Neither do I," he said. "Neither do I."

Feeling considerably better and unwilling to analyze the feeling, she laid her head back against the headrest and watched the countryside go by. They were definitely climbing into the mountains, and even inside the car she could feel the change in the air as it became cooler, thinner. Pine scented the world and the freshness delighted her.

Up and down they drove, slowly through valleys, only to climb again, around hairpin bends. The buttery autumn light cast the woods in gold and made the shadows even more mysterious. This stand of aspens, she thought, must really be out of the way.

Then they emerged over a rise and she gasped with pleasure. A valley appeared to be filled with gold. Brilliant yellow leaves quaked in the breeze, seeming to shimmer and almost emit a light of their own.

"Wow!" No word could adequately describe her reaction to the beauty nestled in this valley. "Just wow!"

"I used to love to take leave in the autumn when I could just to come up here and see this. Want to get out and walk a bit?"

"Absolutely."

Surrounded by the darker green of the firs, the valley made her think of a guarded treasure chest. It was as if the firs coiled around it, like a dragon protecting its hoard.

Fanciful thoughts, strangers to her usually, danced through her mind as they parked near the edge of the aspens then started strolling among them.

The breeze ruffled the leaves, and it almost sounded as if the trees whispered a conversation. She drew deep breaths of the fresh air and felt a smile start to grow throughout her entire body.

"This is incredible," she said.

"Will you be offended if I take your arm? The ground is so uneven."

She gave it a moment's thought. "I don't want to fall," she admitted. "That could be catastrophic."

So he slipped his arm through hers and hugged it to his side. A warm, hard side. Truth to tell, she doubted there was a human on the planet who was any harder physically than a SEAL. All planes, angles and well-honed muscles.

"Do you still work out?" she asked.

"I have to. After all these years, I feel awful if I don't. You?"

"I can still do most everything. No warnings. I've stopped running, though."

"Why?"

"Because I don't seem to have the lung capacity I used to." She laughed quietly. "My friends say I'm carrying high. Which I guess means Junior is taking up some lung space. So I take brisk walks instead. But I've known some women who keep right on running."

"Some of my sisters did. A couple of them gave it up, though. I don't know why. Maybe for the same reason you did." Then he asked, "You call him Junior?"

"That was the first time. Why?"

"I don't know. All I've heard you call him is the baby and the kid."

She flushed faintly. "I guess I've been objectifying him."

"It takes some getting used to" was all he said.

She availed herself of a tree, while he headed back to the car to get some bottled water. "I don't need to tell you about staying hydrated at altitude. We're about eight thousand feet here. I'll be right back."

She had just finished straightening her clothes when he returned carrying a couple of liter bottles. He passed her one and she was surprised to realize that she was truly thirsty. She drained most of it in one draft.

When she lowered the bottle, she found his smiling green-brown eyes on her. "I'm glad I thought of that."

"So am I." She dabbed her lips with her sleeve. "That was good."

"There's plenty more."

They continued their walk, her arm tucked through his, then came to a place where a brook tumbled down a rock face and carved its way back through the forest. There were a couple of good-sized boulders and he suggested a brief rest.

Eight thousand feet, she thought as she perched on one of the rocks. She was feeling it, too. She wondered if that was good. "Could I get altitude sickness here?"

"Not usually at this height, but it can happen. Just don't overexert and keep drinking." He passed her his unopened bottle.

She finished hers and then started on his. "What about you?"

"I'm acclimated. I spent a lot of time hiking up here over the summer. The mining town is lower, so I'd recommend lunching there."

She nodded and looked around at this little piece of heaven. "The aspens are gorgeous. Like bottled sunlight. They're going away?"

"Unfortunately. Each year more die, and they're not spreading. We never had that many to begin with because the climate here is more suited to firs, but I hear they're losing them in Colorado, too."

"And the maples in New England," she added. "I read about that somewhere."

He acknowledged her words with a moment of silence. "Let's get you back to the car. While the altitude isn't that dangerous, I'd feel better about you if we were lower."

So would she, when she thought about it. Seth kept them to a slow pace, but even so she was aware that she was beginning to feel as if she'd run more than a few miles.

She was growing amazingly sleepy again. It happened more often now, and she was resigned to not having her normal level of energy until after the baby was born, but every so often it chafed her. She was used to being active physically, and these new limitations irritated her.

They drove back down winding, hilly roads until at last Seth pulled off onto a narrow, rutted track. "We can't get too close. We had to rope the area off a few years back because some of the old mining tunnels are collapsing. The worst of it is, we're not sure where all the tunnels run."

"What about a ground-penetrating radar?"

He cocked an amused eye at her. "Costs money and the county budget is tight. We're asking the forest service to take over the place, but so far they don't seem eager. Understandable since a decade or so ago they took over a big chunk of ground on and around Thunder Mountain. They're overtaxed. So in the meantime, we just have to be careful and not get too close."

The tumbledown mining site interested her with its echoes of a distant and different past. She would have loved to get close to some of those sagging buildings, to look inside and imagine the kinds of lives people had lived here, but the barriers were up all around, the warning signs plain to see…as were the collapsed mine tunnels, deep pits in the earth. Having the ground give way would have been a dangerous, if not deadly, experience.

They walked around outside the barriers and Seth told her this had once been a favorite place for teens to come. "They could get out of the wind, away from parents. Or, a lot apparently came to get spooked at night. Stories of ghosts abound."

She glanced at him. "You would have liked to grow up here, wouldn't you?"

He shrugged. "I liked where I grew up. No point missing something that wasn't there."

He was right, of course, but she was sure he had to sometimes wonder how different his childhood would have been.

He found a place soft with pine needles a safe distance away and spread out a blanket. A few moments later he returned from the car with some big bags and more water bottles.

She still felt parched and drank thirstily before she even looked at the sandwiches he unwrapped.

After months of telling herself she didn't care about him, didn't care what he did, that she was going ahead with her life alone with a baby, she discovered she was full of questions. Questions she wasn't sure she could ask. But getting to know him seemed important, especially when he'd made it plain that he intended to be part of their child's future.

"I need to know you better," she said lamely, leaving the questions alone for now. She decided to see how forthcoming he would be.

He crossed his legs, put his sandwich on the wrapper and wiped his mouth. "That's reasonable, given the circumstances. What would you like to know?"

"Anything that hasn't been redacted."

He gave her one of those charming smiles that invariably made her heart skip a beat. How the hell did he do that? She supposed that was one question that would never have an answer.

"Well," he said slowly. "I think I had an average childhood, mostly. I was raised by a lovely older couple. Well, they seemed older to me than most of my friends' parents, let me put it that way. But they were super. They never concealed the fact that I was adopted and told me they were luckier than most parents because they got to choose me."

"That's really nice."

He shrugged. "For the times it was unusual. I guess it's more common now, but I'm not exactly in tune with that part of the world. I've been spending too much time being redacted."

That drew a laugh from her. She drank more water and took another bite of her sandwich.

"Even though I knew I was adopted, it didn't seem like a big deal until after they were gone. Then I got this compulsion to find my birth parents." He cocked a brow at her. "That *could* have been a big mistake. I was lucky."

Edie nodded. "They seem like wonderful people."

"Not only wonderful, but despite the fact that my appearance damn near shattered their marriage, they were very welcoming to me. The thing is, getting to know them seemed to fill in parts of me that I hadn't realized were missing. I don't know exactly how to explain it. It's like you suddenly understand something about why you are who you are. I'm not saying it's all genetics, because it's not, but it answers some deep need of some kind. Best I can do."

She thought about it for a few minutes. "I guess I can understand a little. I sometimes wonder how much I'm like my mother, and how much I'm like whoever my father was. My grandmother was able to tell me a lot about my mom, but telling and experiencing aren't the same. And of course, my dad could have been anyone."

"So you became a very self-reliant person."

She tilted her head. "Maybe so. I don't know how much that absence had to do with my choices. I don't know how much my genetics played into it. How could I?"

"But I get the feeling you're determined not to rely on anyone."

She glanced down. "That's true," she admitted. "No more than I have to anyway. I like being in control."

"I get that part. Totally."

She gave him a small smile. "I seem to be a bit out of control now."

He shook his head. "You made decisions. Nobody else made them. Now, unfortunately maybe, I'm mucking up the works for you."

"I don't know about that," she admitted. Oddly, she was losing her appetite, but it had been a large sandwich. She began to wrap the remains. "I guess part of what played into my decision to tell you was not knowing who my father was. I didn't want that to happen to this baby. If nothing else, I had to at least be able to tell him something about you. About the kind of person you are. And I sure didn't ever want to look at him and admit I'd never told you about him."

He surprised her by reaching for her hand and squeezing it. His skin was warm, dry, callused. She wished he'd keep on holding her, but he let go almost immediately. "I'm glad you made those decisions."

"Me, too," she admitted. "I don't know how this is going to work, or even if it will, but I could just imagine the anger from him if I never even told you. He'd be right to get angry. Furious. I would have cheated him."

"So now it's up to me to decide how much he gets cheated?"

She flushed a little. "I didn't mean it that way."

"Maybe not, but that's what it comes down to." He must have read something in her face because he said quickly, "Don't get mad. It's just the bottom line. You were right to tell me. Now it's my decision, at least to some extent. Inevitable. I've already told you I want to be part of the baby's life. We'll have to work it out, but we have to work it out for him."

She looked off toward the mining camp, releasing the annoyance that had started to rise in her. He was right, she had thrown a responsibility directly on his shoulders. Would it have been easier to tell this child his dad wanted no part of him? Would it have caused fewer problems? Not likely.

She sighed and put the wrapped sandwich aside. "Whatever brought me to the decision, I did it."

Her back ached a little, as it sometimes did now, and she stretched out on the blanket with her knees up, staring into pine boughs overhead, catching glimpses of a deep blue sky. It was so peaceful here she wished she could capture it in a bottle and take it with her.

"As for more about me," he said, as if their conversation had become interrupted, "well, you know I've been married twice. The first time I should have listened to my reservations."

"Reservations?"

"Darlene grew up here. She'd never been away from here. I tried to tell her how hard a navy marriage can be. I warned her she'd be in a strange place and I'd be gone for long stretches, that I couldn't even tell her where I'd be or what I'd done when I got back. We actually argued about it more than once."

"So what happened?"

"She told me she could handle it and that I had no right to make her decision for her."

"Hard to argue with that."

"Yeah. Too bad I was right. We didn't make it quite two years. Nobody can imagine it until they've done it. I'd get a call, or get orders that I couldn't even show her, and I'd be gone. I couldn't even tell her when I'd be back. That's a lot to ask of anyone."

She nodded, feeling her eyelids droop a little. "So she couldn't take it."

"She wasn't built that way. I don't know about the air force, but I know navy marriages are tough, even when you know your sailor will only be at sea for six months. With me it was worse. No real information of any kind. It might be a week or two, it might be months, depending. The only things I could tell her had to do with when I'd be training. The only times I could promise to be home for dinner. That's a lot to ask of anyone. But instead of listening to my common sense, I listened to my heart. I loved her."

A simple, straightforward declaration that touched her. "But you did it again."

He snorted. "Yeah, I did it again. Maria was much more mature, and retirement wasn't that far away. Unfortunately..." He didn't finish.

"I'm sorry."

"I'm sorry I lost her, but I'm not sorry we had the time we did. I wouldn't exchange those memories for anything."

She closed her eyes, for some reason feeling close to tears. "That's beautiful."

"It just is. The truth."

She'd never really wished for love before. Career was everything in her life until lately. But just then she wished someone would say that about her someday.

She realized she was hovering on the edge of sleep, her breathing growing slower and steadier. She tried to open her eyes, but her lids felt weighted.

"Take a nap," Seth said quietly. "It's the perfect time and place."

As if she could have done anything else.

Chapter Five

Seth stretched out, too, although he didn't feel the least sleepy, and watched over Edie. Not that there was much here to protect her from, but it made him feel good.

He wondered if he were about to make another big mistake. He couldn't deny that he still felt the same attraction to her that had led him to her table in the ramshackle officers club at the air base in Afghanistan. He'd told himself it was just because he wanted to thank her—that had been some flying job—but even now he could remember other things pulling him her way.

She sat alone, for one thing, as if she didn't want to get into the sometimes juvenile hijinks that occurred when people were blowing off steam and adrenaline. She appeared to have surrounded herself in a cocoon of composure, the same composure she had displayed in the cockpit. As if she wanted nothing to touch her or ruffle her calm.

He could get that part, and that wasn't what had pulled him. No, what had pulled him was simple sexual attraction. Gut male urges that he honestly hadn't expected to act on. But that didn't mean he couldn't enjoy a beautiful woman's company for the evening.

And she was beautiful, for all she tried to hide it

with that ridiculously short haircut and behind cammies. Beautiful to him at any rate.

And she still pulled him in the same basic way. He wanted her again. Remembering how much fun she'd been beforehand…well, he could understand why she wasn't feeling like a whole lot of fun right now. That didn't matter. So far he liked her well enough. And he wanted her like hell. Still.

Wow.

He'd made love to her five months ago, yet he could still remember how she looked naked, how her warm skin had felt beneath his hands, how responsive she had been. He felt a twinge of guilt even now that he had been her first. Surely a woman deserved better than a hurried mating for her first time. But she had said she hadn't regretted it. He couldn't help wondering if she still felt that way. *Really* felt that way.

One thing for sure, he'd been the one with the greater experience and he should have known better than to indulge. However much he had wanted her, he had known exactly what it might be: a one-night stand. Yeah, he'd hoped she'd get in touch, but he hadn't expected it. And while that was okay for some people, it wasn't okay for all of them. He should never have given in to his hunger for her.

He felt a little ashamed of his own lack of control—after all, that was something he prided himself on—but he'd lost control because of a red-haired, blue-eyed witch.

He laughed silently as he folded his hands behind his head and stared up at the trees and sky. He somehow suspected she would hate him for thinking of her as a witch. But he meant that in the best way possible. She'd cast a spell of some kind over him, and he'd misbehaved.

Now there were consequences to deal with. Just how he was going to deal with them he couldn't imagine. She probably didn't want him to become a permanent fixture in her life, so he guessed he was going to be doing a lot of traveling to see his son, because he wasn't going to allow that boy to grow up without him. No way on earth.

While he had no experience of being a father, he had been blessed with two good fathers as examples. And he supposed he'd get plenty of advice from Marge…and Nate, come to that, if Marge pressed him. Or if he asked.

He could do this. Everybody had to ease into having a first baby, so he'd have time to learn. And he had always wanted a kid or two. With Maria, they'd wanted two. They'd never gotten to the point of actually doing it, but they had talked about it.

Now it was on the way and he needed to think about things like how much he could be there, and even how to change a diaper. Damn, to think that at his age he'd never done that. When his sisters came home, he was allowed to hold the babies, but the minute one needed changing or feeding, it was swiped from his arms. He guessed he'd been judged inadequate, being childless. Amusement twisted his mouth. That was about to change.

Of course, what he might discover was that the major force in his family—the women—might take over for him. They'd certainly try, and he'd have more advice than a single man could use. Assuming, of course, that Edie allowed him to actually care for the child.

Thinking about it, though, daunting as parts seemed, he felt a true longing for this child. An unexpected gift when he'd about given up on the whole idea. When he'd envisioned the rest of his life as solitary and self-contained except for his family.

Damn, the truth was, he still wasn't a civilian. Not completely. He was getting better at acting the part, but long years of training and dangerous experience had made him into something that didn't quite fit with what most people considered ordinary life.

But he could probably say the same for the woman napping beside him. They were both about to embark on the unknown, something for which neither of them had any training or experience to guide them.

Maybe the most important thing they would ever do, when you came right down to it.

She stirred beside him, but before he could look to see if she had awakened, she rolled over, murmuring softly, and threw her arm across him. The next thing he knew, her head was resting in the hollow of his shoulder.

He almost held his breath, afraid of waking her. It had been so long since a woman had turned to him this way in her sleep and he didn't want to lose these fragile moments. They could get back to distrusting, arguing, hammering things out later.

For now he just wanted to enjoy the illusion created by a woman's arm around him and a woman's head on his shoulder.

The illusion that he really wasn't alone.

A chill down her back slowly woke Edie. She felt as if she were emerging from some deep, dark place that she couldn't quite climb out of. But the chill wouldn't leave her alone, and then she noticed that while her neck and back were cold, her front wasn't.

Huh?

She jerked awake and realized she had wrapped herself around Seth. At once her cheeks flamed. "Oh! I'm sorry!"

"I didn't mind," he said quietly.

When she raised her head, she saw no smile there, no amusement, simply a kind of quietude.

"I'm getting a little cold," she said, resisting the ridiculous urge to just burrow into him again. He might be warm, but her back wasn't, and how much more trouble did she want anyway?

"Let's get you home, then."

Home? she thought as she stood up. She didn't have a home. He probably meant his house or his parents' house, but either way it was not her home. For years now her home had been a series of rooms in various air bases, like moving motel to motel. It had been a long time since she had called any place home in a meaningful sense.

She looked down at her stomach, rested her hand on her growing child and wondered why she hadn't thought of that before. Did she want him to grow up rootless, moving from base to base, housing unit to housing unit? At least she'd had the stability of her grandmother's house. The stability of never moving from the time she turned three until she left high school.

That had to mean something.

"Everything okay?" Seth asked. He had put the remains of lunch away in the bags and now folded the blanket. The shadows had grown long while she slept and the air had taken on a distinct chill.

"No," she said slowly. "Just thinking."

His expression was questioning, but she didn't answer. She'd left a big piece out of this puzzle and she couldn't ignore its absence any longer. Damn, did she need to leave her job, too?

The thought didn't cheer her at all. But, she reminded herself, there were plenty of military brats, after all. Apparently it wasn't all bad.

But still...

The thought plagued her all the way back to town, and she realized that part of her wasn't going to leave it alone. She had to think and make a decision, a decent decision. The best one she could for the baby.

This whole pregnancy thing was eating her alive. But there it was. Real, growing, and soon to be a very-much-present baby with needs that couldn't be provided through an umbilical cord.

She kept her face averted, watching the countryside pass, watching the night creep over the world. What in the world had ever made her think she could be a good mother?

Her emotions had roamed nearly the entire compass over the past few months, but now they had headed in an entirely different direction. After convincing herself she could do this, now uncertainty filled her.

She lived like a gypsy and had since the day she left for officer training. She basically lived out of a duffel. She knew nothing about raising a child. Hell, she'd only changed a few diapers in her life, back in high school the few times she had babysat.

"What exactly am I offering a child?" She didn't realize the words had emerged until she heard Seth's response.

"A dedicated mother."

She swung her head around, aware that her eyes had grown hot—damn tears, always so near the surface now—and looked at him. "That's not enough. Do I have to tell you how I live? Is that good for a kid? Is it?"

He didn't answer immediately, and with each passing second she felt as if another stone dropped into her heart. "I know military couples with kids. The love moves with them even if the place changes. And you know it's basically a small community at heart. You change bases and meet up with people you knew from a base or two ago."

"Maybe. How would I know? I'm not living the family life. I'm not even sure I'm capable of it."

Another pause, then he said, "Like I said, everybody starts out utterly inexperienced. There's no real preparation for being a parent. I think you know that. All the advice in the world isn't the same as reality. So what's really worrying you?"

"That I'm rootless. You said you'd take me home, and I realized I haven't had a home in a long time. Not a real home. Now I have to figure out how to make one. I'm not sure I know how."

"I could hand you some clichés, but that won't work. I can totally get where you're coming from. I tried a couple of times to make my own home, but I was gone more than I was there. After Maria, I even thought it might be a damn good thing that we hadn't made a baby yet."

"And now look." Her laugh was harsh. "You're getting a baby ready or not. I thought I had it all settled. Damn it, Seth, there are a million things I didn't even think about. Like not living out of my duffel anymore. That just won't work. And even if I stay stateside, I can't guarantee I won't be bouncing around every couple of years. You know how that goes. Training squadron? Yeah, they're based at one place now. That could change. And even so, there'd be temporary assignments, refreshers to take at other bases. Plenty of temporary duty assignments."

"I know." She could tell he didn't see the point in arguing against the obvious. "Well, I could step in."

"Yeah. I'll bring the baby here, disrupt his life for a few months, then come back and disrupt it again. I've got to figure this out."

He didn't argue.

"My place or my parents'?" he asked as they reached the edge of town.

"Yours," she said quietly. "I don't think I'm up to your mother just now."

He laughed quietly. "She can be overwhelming."

"I like her, really. But I don't want any pressure right now. Just my luck that she'd put her finger on the very things I'm worrying about."

"She can be good at that."

He turned onto his dimly lit street. "You can stay the night and take my bed. I'll get some dinner for us, and we can just relax and chat about whatever you like. Or if you want, I have some books you can read. Do you want me to run over to my folks' house to get your stuff?"

"If you wouldn't mind. I don't want to insult them, but…"

"I'll just explain we need privacy to talk. No offense. Promise."

She hesitated as he put the car into Park. "Where will you sleep?"

"On the floor. I've slept in places a whole lot worse, believe me."

She had no trouble believing it at all. She'd slept in a few herself. She felt briefly guilty about it then told herself to cut it out. He could stay with his parents if he didn't want to sleep on the floor.

She just knew she couldn't go back there. Just her brief exposure had reminded her of a life she had never really known. As loving as her grandmother had been, it had still been life with an elderly person, no rambunctious siblings or cousins. Almost monastic in a way.

Yeah, she was going to make one hell of a mother.

Seth had a couple of relatively new easy chairs in his living room, signs of occupancy. He probably spent a lot of time here, and the extra chair indicated he sometimes had a friend or family member over.

She settled into one, wondering if the internal wrestling match would ever be over. She thought she'd worked this all out, and now she was facing a new problem. Having a baby was a big deal. Having one when you were rootless was an even bigger deal.

It was all well and good for her to consider her unit her home, the air force her community, but while that worked for an adult, she wasn't so sure about a child.

Seth had made a good point about how the love would travel with them wherever they went, but would that be enough? Just her and a baby? And those stints of temporary duty really worried her for the first time. How could she have not thought about them before?

Because she still hadn't really dealt with all the life changes that were coming. Much as she wanted to plan and prepare and be ready for everything, she hadn't had time to consider every single thing yet. It felt as if new considerations just kept popping up.

Like this one. She once again had been thinking in terms of fitting the baby into her life, not fitting her life around the baby. Stupid.

A child would be utterly dependent on her for everything. It was not a matter of fitting this baby into her life, it had to be the other way around. It had to be.

So maybe it was time to start thinking about that. Maybe her career was no longer a viable option.

The thought sat like a lead weight in her stomach. What would she do? What kind of life could she build that she would love as much as the one she already had?

Although if she were to be honest, some of the shine had come off that, especially lately when she saw her future narrowing. She hadn't been picked for combat search and rescue, she had volunteered for it and sought it. Now that was gone.

Which left what? Teaching others to do what she loved and always hankering to get back to it? Or something else? The problem was, she had never thought of doing something else. Since the day she had first heard of CSAR, it was all she had wanted to do.

Of course, a realistic view of life would tell her that even without a baby those days were numbered. A great many pilots were removed from combat duty in their early thirties for a variety of reasons. Sooner or later, they would have yanked her back anyway.

So it was just a little sooner. She'd cope, because she had to. But she admitted to herself that she was woefully unprepared to consider the question. It had always lurked somewhere in her future, but she hadn't given it a thought anyway. It would have hit her like a ton of bricks regardless.

She thought of other pilots she'd seen get the results of their flight physicals only to hear that some little quirk, a quirk that wasn't causing problems, had showed up on the electrocardiograms. Or some other thing. It didn't matter, it was always something minor that wouldn't affect them in any important way, but they were no longer considered fit for combat flying. They could only fly trainers after that. She'd felt for them, but honestly hadn't been able to imagine how much that would hurt. Until now. Now she felt it all the way to her soul.

All of a sudden her future, which had steadily been shifting shape, now became one great big blank.

Of course, Seth thought as he picked up Edie's belongings, everything was already neatly packed in her duffel. Nothing left out on bathroom counters, by the tub, beside the bed. Ready to go at an instant's notice. He couldn't help smiling crookedly as he saw it. How long had he lived the same way? Even during his marriages, that damn duffel had been there, ready to go.

Big changes. He was beginning to sense what was troubling Edie. She hadn't expected to face these changes for a while yet, but they were barreling down on her right now. He could sympathize, at least to some extent.

After all, he'd opted to retire rather than take a training or desk assignment. Given his rank, it would have been mostly behind a desk. But he'd had time to make mental adjustments. He'd been making them for the last few years. Edie was trying to do it in a matter of months.

"Why didn't she come stay here?"

Seth turned to see Marge in the doorway. "We need time, Mom. Private time, that's all. We've got a lot to work out."

Marge bit her lower lip. "She does know she's welcome?"

"Of course she knows. She's probably overwhelmed

by the welcome. I think she expected to be turned away, not have an entire family laid at her feet."

Marge smiled a bit. "We can overwhelm, can't we?"

"I'm still getting used to it myself. Relax. We just need the time. Big changes and all that."

"I suppose. But, Scth, how can you be a single parent while you're on active duty?"

Seth bent and lifted the duffel. "You'd be surprised what people can do. Let *us* work it out, and don't say things that might offend Edie."

"I'd never do that!"

"Not intentionally. This woman is extremely competent. She'll make the right decisions."

"They'd better include you."

"They already are."

With that he managed to escape the house. He could well understand why Edie didn't want to come back. Marge was rushing her fences, full of questions and probably solutions. But Edie, and he, had to answer their own questions. Nobody else could make it right for both of them.

He stopped at the diner and tried to pick up enough food to get them through morning. That kitchen of his wasn't good for cooking yet, and he hadn't gotten very many utensils. He threw in a big salad for good measure, figuring a pregnant woman needed healthy food. Then he hit the grocery fast for milk, crackers, cheese, fruit and some sweet rolls. Damn, he didn't even know what Edie liked to eat.

The learning curve was getting about as steep as his BUD/S training had been. That brought a grin to his lips. Another mountain to conquer, even if it was inside himself. He'd been facing down those mountains and cliffs for a long time. Challenge was a great thing.

When he got back he found Edie sitting in a recliner with her feet up. Still wearing boots. He managed to hide his smile about that. She was ready to jump and go on a moment's notice. He figured that he'd win a major victory the day he could get her to sit around here in stocking feet.

She smiled faintly when she saw him. "Everything go okay?"

"Mom was understanding, but I can tell you, you were right not to want to go back tonight. She wants to rush a bunch of solutions."

"She seems like someone who likes to solve problems."

"Must run in the family. Sorry I took so long, but I decided that given the baby I'd better buy some groceries, not just Maude's food. I got some salad there, but stopped to pick up milk and a few other things for nibbles. Then it struck me I don't even know what you like."

"I think we had this discussion. Life didn't make me a picky eater."

He gave a laugh. "Me neither. But there are probably nutritional rules you need to be following."

"At the mess hall I don't have to think about it much. Everything is there."

"Well, it's not here, so you'll have to guide me." He turned. "I still need to bring in the groceries." He dropped her duffel by the door. "At least I have a working fridge."

He returned to his vehicle and pulled out the cloth bags. Inside he found Edie in the kitchen now, ready to help him. She opened the fridge and started to laugh.

"It's pretty embarrassing," he admitted.

"A six-pack? You really don't eat here."

"Not very often. I have a permanent dinner invitation with Mom and Dad, and sometimes my sisters step in."

"How many of them live here?"

"Just two, Mary and Wendy. The rest are scattered over the country. Thanksgiving and Christmas bring the herd home."

"What do they do?" she asked as she helped move groceries into the refrigerator.

"Mary's a nurse at the hospital. She did a tour in the navy for a while, then with the VA. And Wendy is a flight nurse. She and her husband run our county emergency response team." He paused. "I think you'd like her husband, Yuma. He flew Hueys in Vietnam and now he flies them for our emergency response team."

She sat slowly on a chair. "Really?"

"Really."

"That's some family you got there."

"I think so. Some of my sisters are nurses, some are teachers. By the time you add in husbands, we've got cops, doctors, journalists."

"Overwhelming."

"Only until you get used to it. Take Mary. You couldn't ask for a sweeter, kinder person."

"And Wendy?"

"She's a little tougher in her own way. I mean, Mary dealt with the Asian tsunami cleanup, and a lot of severely wounded vets. I suspect she's got a few nightmares, but you'd never guess. Wendy, though...well, she got tough a different way, chasing Yuma."

That surprised a laugh from Edie. "How would that toughen her?"

"She fell in love with him when she was still a kid. He wanted no part of it. He had a lot of PTSD and a drinking problem. For a while he even lived up in the mountains with a bunch of other vets who had really severe PTSD. Anyway, Wendy didn't give up. She went to work in a big-city emergency room so she could understand some of what Yuma was dealing with, then she came back here a grown woman and just refused to listen to his nonsense. She'd made up her mind. Even got involved with the vets in the mountains."

"She sounds like something else."

"There's little that will divert her once she makes up her mind. You know, I bet Yuma would let you take the stick of one of our ERT Hueys, if you want."

"I'd love that!"

He smiled. "I figured. I'll see."

Watching her dig into the salad did his heart good. As he had suspected, she needed more than sandwiches, and she really hadn't had anything else all day. She also downed two glasses of milk. He made mental notes. Likely it wasn't all that different from a good training diet.

He insisted on cleaning up and told her to go relax and, "For God's sake, take off those boots."

At that she giggled, a sound he hadn't heard since that night in Afghanistan so long ago. She had laughed a few times since arriving here, but nothing that sounded quite as free as that giggle. Well, with the possible exception of when she saw what was in his fridge.

He knew, though, that something new had started to bother her that afternoon on the way back from the mountains, and he wondered how the hell he could find out. She wasn't talking much yet, not that he could blame her. They'd shared the greatest of intimacies, had even created a life, yet they didn't know each other at all, really. Perfect strangers. That didn't create much of a climate for a heart-to-heart.

Although he wasn't sure how good he was with that kind of thing. Neither of his marriages had been long enough to really test his ability to talk with a woman about difficult things...with the exception of one screaming match as a woman walked out the door.

He'd spent most of his adult life dealing with other men in special ops. He knew those rules, knew you could be closer than brothers and still not say some things. Ever.

He hadn't been around his sisters enough over the years under circumstances that would have helped him make up for his shortfalls. But maybe talking to a woman wasn't all that different. Maybe he just needed to be honest and find his way through.

Hell if he knew. All of a sudden he felt as if he had missed half of life's necessary experiences.

When he went to the living room, he found that Edie had at last removed her boots. "How are your ankles?"

"Growing by the second."

"Is that bad?"

"Not really. It's only really bad if I spend all day standing or sitting. I didn't do that today. The swelling will be minor."

"Anything special you need to do for it?"

"Keep my feet up."

He sat in the facing chair and waited. He had the worst urge to touch her, even if it was only to massage her ankles. Damn, it was too soon to be thinking of such

things, if it would ever be possible again. A thought occurred to him.

"Do you feel like I betrayed you?"

Her eyes widened. "I told you I didn't blame you.
We're adults, Seth. You even used protection."

"But I was gone the next morning. I never wrote or
anything."

"You gave me your parents' address. You'll notice I
didn't try to reach you, either, until…well."

"Yeah. But I still feel a little guilty. I mean, I'm used
to having to take off that way. We didn't hold still for
long. But…unless you're used to that it could seem cold."

"I understood. I've been around that block a few
times. I get missions and orders. I know."

One advantage to a woman who had shared the lifestyle.

"But I've been thinking about that," she said, pulling
his entire attention to her.

"About what?" he asked when she remained silent.

"I may have to resign my commission."

He didn't like the sinking feeling that hit him in the
gut. "Edie…" The protest was instinctive. He knew how
hard he'd worked for his goals, and he didn't for a second doubt she had worked every bit as hard. To just toss
it all away?

But she shook her head. "I haven't decided. But while
you were out it struck me that I've been thinking about
all the ways I can fit this baby into my life. I haven't
given any thought at all to how I can fit my life to this
baby and what's best for him."

He honestly didn't know how to respond to that. What
good would it do to toss off easy suggestions about how
he could fill in when necessary? He suspected that

wasn't what she was trying to get at. There was something deeper going on here.

One thought did occur to him, and he spoke it, knowing it might well infuriate her. "Just don't give up so much that you immolate yourself on a pyre of self-denial."

"Meaning?"

"A bitter mother is hardly better than no mother at all. You don't want to hate this kid because he cost you everything."

For an instant, he thought she was going to erupt. He could have sworn he saw blue fire leap in her eyes. Who was he, after all, to say anything about her decisions? But a few seconds later she sighed and closed her eyes. "You're right. And that's part of what's making this so hard."

"Anything else?"

"What?"

"Is something else pushing you on these decisions? Because I'm sure not every one of them needs to be made right away. I mean, some can be decided after the baby comes when you see how things are working. He's not likely to remember much of his first few months except whether he feels secure."

"True." She still didn't open her eyes. "Maybe I'm wondering these things because my own mother stunk at motherhood. She didn't care enough to give up drugs."

He hesitated. "Did they affect you?"

"No. Apparently not. From everything my grandmother said, I wasn't born addicted. I guess she didn't really get hooked herself until after I came along."

"Or maybe she cared enough not to mess you up while she carried you."

Edie's eyes snapped open. He couldn't read her expression at all. He wished he were a mind reader. "It's possible," she said finally. "I don't know much. Anything's possible."

"Cling to that thought. It's better than other possibilities."

"Are you always an optimist?"

"I couldn't have done all that redacted stuff if I weren't."

Her eyes widened, then a genuine, delightful laugh escaped her. "That's so true! Same here."

He grinned. "I love your laugh."

The words seemed to hang in the air, stilling it, quieting even the quiet house. Her expression changed, but he couldn't read it, and he hoped he hadn't just put his foot in it big-time, although he couldn't imagine how.

"Thanks," she said finally. It was almost noncommittal.

Now where to go? She didn't want to be pressured, understandably, but he had a stake in this, and realized that it was growing more important to him by the hour. "This baby thing?" he said finally, hoping he wouldn't say it all wrong.

"Yes?"

"I'm starting to really like the idea. Next thing I'll be buying catcher's mitts and baseball bats."

Another laugh escaped her, but it wasn't as light and easy. "Too soon."

"I think," he said slowly, "that was kind of my point. Not everything has to be decided before the baby comes. A general outline would be great, but some of this is just going to have to be flying by the seat of the pants. It must be for everyone."

She let her head fall back and closed her eyes. At least she wasn't angry. "I guess I'm trying to deal with this like a mission, take care of all the details ahead of time. And I don't even know what all the details are yet."

"No," he agreed.

She popped open one eye. "You're serious? You really like the idea of the baby?"

"I really do. More and more as I think about it. So much so that I hope you and I can work out ways to give him the best life possible. I definitely want to be a part of it. As big a part as you'll allow."

She stunned him then with a challenge that sounded almost angry. "So then let's get married and create that nice little family you're imagining!"

He stared at her.

She laughed and the sound was edgy. "Right. This is always going to be clear skies and sailing. Just patch a few holes in the boat and everything will be right."

A certainty settled over him. "Okay."

Her jaw dropped and now both her eyes opened. "Cut it out."

"I'm serious. I'll marry you tomorrow. Give the boy a name. A father."

"Oh, for God's sake, Seth! Don't be ridiculous. You don't know me and I don't know you, and damn it, it would just make things messier. You ought to know that!"

"Messier how? It wouldn't be the first marriage of convenience. Having a father to look after the child could salvage your career. I'll go wherever you go and give the boy a stable home. If we discover we can't stand it, well, maybe divorce wouldn't be as bad for the kid as not trying at all."

She swore. "You've lost your mind!"

"I don't think so. Damn it, Edie, I married twice for love. The first time turned into hell anyway. The second…well, I'm not keen to go through that kind of pain again. So why not do it for the kid? We'd set our boundaries, take care of the baby and maybe just be good friends. You could still have your career. The kid gets a stable home. Think you can't tough it out for twenty years? Somehow I doubt that, given what you've done with your life."

"Toughing it out isn't my idea of marriage."

"Maybe not. But what are the risks compared to what we're considering now? Minimal for you and me. Better for the baby."

"If we don't fight like cats and dogs."

He shook his head. "I've got more self-control than that. I think you do, too. So consider this my proposal. Save your career, give the baby the home you're worrying about, and we'll deal with each other as two people on a mission."

"Damn, doesn't that sound like a SEAL."

One corner of his mouth lifted, although he didn't at all feel like smiling. "Think like a pilot. You want to plan the mission? This is the biggest missing piece."

She slammed the recliner footrest down and stood up. "I'm going to bed. And you're insane."

He watched her walk down the hall to his bedroom, then sat back in his own chair. Well, he'd sure riled her.

But he didn't think he was insane.

Chapter Six

Edie didn't sleep much. So much for being sleepier as the pregnancy progressed. She tossed and turned, feeling as if Seth had opened a whole new can of worms when she was already trying to deal with a dozen of them.

She also felt as if Mephistopheles were whispering in her ear, tempting her with promises of a return to a seminormal career, of rising again as she had hoped to rise, of returning to flight status and combat status, the chance to once again rescue her comrades in their hour of need.

A devil's temptation, she thought. Sell her soul for her career? But would it even be selling her soul?

Her confusion and distress reached new heights. She tried to calm herself down for the sake of the child. She understood that her stress could be bad for the baby. But hell, she'd been stressed continuously for months now. What was a little more?

Seth was nuts. A marriage of convenience? Seriously?

But it tempted her. To know that so many details would be taken care of, that the stability she worried about for the child would be provided, yeah, it was tempting.

It was still crazy.

She was sure he was imagining something like the

family he'd found with the Tates. Perhaps like his adoptive family. Apparently he had a good background that way. Her, not so much. She hadn't the foggiest idea how to manage it.

So what the hell was she doing having a baby anyway?

Frustrated, angry, scared, when she got up in the morning, she packed her duffel and headed for the door. She was going back to base. She'd deal with this by herself, because somehow that felt better than letting anyone else step in. Her overwhelming need for control, she supposed. Part of what made her a damn good pilot.

She didn't get to the front door before she was blocked by Seth. "Running?" he asked casually.

"From a crazy man. I need space."

"I'll give it to you here, but I'm not letting you go."

"You can't keep me."

He put his hands on his narrow hips and stared her down. "Damn it, Edie, you know running never fixed a thing. You're the last person on this planet I would expect to flee. You've faced down a helluva lot more than me making a suggestion that marriage might be a solution."

"Shotgun marriages don't work."

"Then say no and I'll drop it."

God! She opened her mouth but the word wouldn't come out. Damn it, it was as if temptation had cast a spell over her. And it wasn't just about her job, she realized, it was about a damnably attractive guy who she still felt pulled toward as if he were a lodestone. A guy who had broken down years of barriers, taken her to places she couldn't have even imagined, all in a hurried quickie in a ramshackle room on the other side of the world.

She dropped her duffel. Anger at herself swamped her. She was not like this. She was *not*. She was always decisive, always figured out her plans, always handled things. And all of a sudden she didn't want to handle anything. Not one more thing.

"Aw, hell," Seth said, his entire posture softening. It was only then that she realized tears had begun to run down her face.

She wanted to turn away, to hide them, but before she could do so he closed the distance, wrapped his arms around her and carried her to a recliner. He placed her on his lap, tipped back and wound her in his strong embrace, just holding her.

"Shh," he murmured softly, and to her amazement she felt him stroke her hair. "It's been hell for you. But you're not alone now."

That broke through the last of her resistance and the tears began to run freely. For the first time in a long time, sobs ripped through her. For the first time in a long time she honestly felt that she might not be alone.

She wanted to rail against the weakness, but she couldn't. It just felt so damn good to be held, to be with someone who was sharing the problems. The tough exterior she'd built in a man's world was crumbling, and it frightened her, but it felt good, too.

"I never cry," she hiccupped. "At least not until I got pregnant."

"I cry sometimes," he said quietly. "Everyone needs to, once in a while."

The sobbing eased, but the tears continued for a while longer. Months of stress, anguish, worry…all of it seemed to be pouring out through her eyes. Seth continued to hold her close, as if trying to let her know he cared and was there with her.

But how could he care? He didn't know her. Or maybe in some ways he did. He certainly didn't seem to dislike her. She dashed at her eyes, wiped her face on her sleeve, but when she tried to sit up he wouldn't let her.

"Just rest. Just let the calm come. You know how to do it. You've been calm in worse situations."

He was right. She drew a deep breath and sought that familiar place that always accompanied her when she climbed into a cockpit. That wasn't so hard. And it did feel so good to lie against him with her head on his chest, listening to his steady heartbeat. Never had she done that before. Never.

"So the baby is moving, right?" he asked.

"Plenty. Very active little guy."

"Can I feel it sometime?"

Since the baby was now poking her gently—a foot or a hand, she didn't know—she took his hand and placed it over the spot where she could feel the small pressure. After a few moments, he said, "Wow!"

"Yeah," she agreed, her voice rusty. "It's amazing."

And it was. She loved it. If there was one thing she loved about this whole situation, it was feeling that life inside her. Every movement was a reminder, a promise, a joy. It was only when she got buried in the other stuff that she lost sight of the joy.

"You know," he said, with his hand still on her belly to feel the stirring baby, "it's not every day a guy gets a proposal from an ace pilot."

That drew a weak laugh from her. "I was being sarcastic."

"I know. But I wasn't."

She caught her breath, feeling that sinuous pull of her attraction to him. She tried to tug away from it, but that was hard to do when she was lying in his lap and against his chest this way. Damn, he even smelled good, like fresh air and soap. And like man. Never before had she allowed herself to appreciate that last scent, but she was appreciating it now. Desires she had kept in cold storage except for one night were thawing again. Damn, that would only complicate things. She fought around for something else to think of.

"Don't you believe in love?" she asked him finally.

"Absolutely. It's a wonderful thing. I've been in love twice. But if there's one thing I've learned, it takes more than love to make a relationship. You can start with love or not, but in the long run you need friendship, trust, understanding, patience. Hell, Edie, I know from experience that marriage is a lot of work, much of it unexpected. Getting all dewy-eyed at the start won't change that. I've watched my parents work at it. I've had to work at it."

"But why do the work without love?"

"Maybe because you have a kid. Anyway, I'm not pressuring you, but I meant it. I'll marry you today, tomorrow or six months from now. My main point is that you've been dealing with this all on your own for months now. You're not alone any longer. I'll do everything I possibly can to help."

"Thank you," she said finally. Her voice cracked. God, she hated that she felt so weak right now, so alone, so overwhelmed. What had happened to that woman who had come marching out here to do her duty and then skedaddle? Yet lying here like this, she felt an ache of need for what Seth was offering: not to have to face all this by herself.

Weakness? Or good sense?

Almost as if he had read her mind, he remarked, "How many people do you rely on when you get in your helo? Ground crew, maintenance, copilot, door gunner…" He trailed off, letting her think about it. A few minutes later he added, "Yes, you take the responsibility as pilot, but you're relying on others to do their share. We all do. Hell, I had a whole team. We were as tightly knotted in our dependency on each other as a rat's nest, only as good as our weakest link. If we're really honest with ourselves, none of us gets through life truly alone. Well except maybe for a hermit, and somebody has to bring him food."

That drew another small laugh from her. She thought about what he was saying, though, and realized his points were valid. There was a difference between shouldering responsibility and depending on no one else. A huge difference.

He lifted his hand from her belly and gave her a gentle squeeze. "We'll figure it out, Major. That's what we're trained to do after all."

Seth got her to change out of her cammies and into her few civvies, and put her duffel back in his bedroom.

"Just promise me," he said, "promise me that you won't try to take off again for a week or two. You have the leave time."

She suddenly recalled that he'd had a woman walk out on him before. Hadn't she just faced that yesterday when they had their minifight in the car? What had she been thinking and why did she keep trying to run?

Maybe that was the question that she should be pondering. Did she fear she might give him more of herself than he would want? That she would come to care and thus get hurt? If so, she had just won the chicken award.

She didn't run from things. At least not until this. God, she was turning into a wimp. She stiffened her spine. "Then I need some more clothes. Unless you have a washer I can use every night."

"Waste of water. Want to go back to Freitag's and see if you can find something else you like enough to wear?"

At least it would change the subject and give her something else to think about for an hour. Maternity clothes. She was still having trouble with that.

"It's not far. Can we walk? Because I really need the exercise."

He smiled. "Of course. And I'll help carry things back."

The quiet streets enchanted her. Big old trees, changing before the winds of late fall, created a near-tunnel over the sidewalks. The houses, most of them small and older, showed a lot of loving care for the most part, although the lawns would have failed inspection on a military base.

But she liked it, liked the cool, dry breeze, the rustling of those changing leaves, the sense of peace that permeated the place. "Does anything happen around here?"

"Oh, yeah. Every so often my dad used to announce that the place was going to hell in a handbasket."

"When he was sheriff?"

"Yeah. Things happen here the way they happen anywhere. Most people here are good people, though. Great neighbors. If it was ever any more peaceful than it is now, I wouldn't know. Sometimes I think Dad was exaggerating, but obviously I have a different metric."

"To say the least." She looked at him from the corner of her eye. Damn, he was handsome. It was as if his life had honed him to near perfection. Every single time she wasn't worrying the issue of the baby, the attraction slammed her again. If she wasn't careful, a one-night stand could turn into multiple nights. She wasn't sure she could handle that.

The thought of his suggestion of a marriage of convenience wafted through her mind again. She wanted to quash it immediately, for fear she might seize it as an easy solution that would turn out to be anything but easy. But the idea drew her almost as much as he did. Still, some part of her rebelled at turning the raising of their child into a mission. A mission? Shouldn't it be something more than that?

Yet what was a mission, really? A duty, an act of necessity at great risk to accomplish a stated goal. Why should life be any different? She almost sighed. "So you're thinking about becoming a deputy?"

"I don't know," he said frankly. "I'm still working my way back to being a civilian. I have a built-in hair trigger after all these years. I'm not certain that would be the best thing in law enforcement."

"So you need time."

"Some, anyway. We're both going through major changes. I'm sure you get it."

Indeed she did.

As they drew nearer to the downtown, she noticed that the houses increased in size, big gracious buildings from before the Second World War. Not huge, by any means, but they struck her as solid and enduring, unlike much of what she'd known in her life. The street grew a little wider, the lawns a little better tended. Yet still no one was out and about except for a rare passing car. Folks around here must work or be very busy somehow. The quiet of the place, the peacefulness of it, called to her. She'd known little enough of it over the years.

They were approaching Freitag's when a woman of about forty with shaggy, short, blond-streaked hair accosted them. She wore a blue flight suit and called out, "Hey, bro, what's the rush?"

The woman turned out to be Wendy Yuma, Seth's sister, the flight nurse he had mentioned.

"You must be Edie Clapton," Wendy said warmly after Seth introduced her.

So the news was out, Edie realized. Well, of course she couldn't have expected Marge Tate to keep quiet among the family. Her stomach fluttered. Or maybe it was the baby. "Nice to meet you."

"Nice to meet you, too." Wendy smiled as they shook hands. "I haven't got a whole lot of time. I need to get back to the station. How about we do dinner at my place a soon as I can figure out when the schedule is clear? Barring an emergency, that is. Are you guys going to the diner?"

Edie flushed faintly. "I need some more clothes."

"Well, good luck at Freitag's. They have some maternity stuff but not much. Mainly because the mothers around here exchange it constantly. I hope you're not into froufrou because they don't have it."

"I noticed yesterday. And I hate froufrou."

"Good." Wendy's smile widened.

"Say," Seth said, "do you suppose Yuma would give

Edie a chance to fly one of the Hueys? She flies Pave Hawks right now."

Wendy's brow lifted. "CSAR, huh? I bet you he would. And you ought to have plenty to talk about. Yuma flew medevacs in 'Nam. I'll give you a call. Nice meeting you, Edie." Then she hurried off.

"She's nice," Edie remarked, looking after her before resuming the walk that had now taken them to the main street. Freitag's was half a block ahead. "Why does she call her husband by his last name?"

"Because he prefers it. His given name is Billy Joe. Wendy calls him that once in a while but she's the only one."

"Interesting. She looks a bit like your mom."

"But not as pushy," Seth said wryly.

"Your mom's not pushy. She's just…" Edie sought a nicer word.

"Pushy," Seth repeated. "She's been a mother too long."

Edie laughed quietly. "I guess that would do it."

"With six daughters? About like being a pilot or a SEAL, I think."

That drew an even louder laugh from her. "I guess we're going to find out."

As soon as the words popped out, she realized how they might sound. She stole a glance at Seth, but he seemed not to have noticed. After a moment she relaxed again. If he'd taken it the wrong way, he could call her on it. Otherwise, she'd just forget it.

This time he didn't wait near the front of the store, but followed her back to the maternity section. "Use my arms to throw things over if you like them," he said easily.

She hesitated. "Seth, people might talk."

"They probably already are. And they're good at putting two and two together, believe me."

She hadn't thought about that possibility, but standing there faced by racks of maternity clothes, she realized that it was inevitable. She had bought maternity clothes yesterday. She was staying with Seth. What would be the most obvious conclusion to draw?

"Do you...do you mind?" she asked carefully.

"Hell, no. I'm sure I've already been cast as the villain in the piece, the unscrupulous user of innocent women who will now pay for his sins. At least they won't be bored for a few days."

He gave her a breathtaking grin. She giggled. "So we're a soap opera?"

"Pretty darn near."

"I'd rather be cast as the evil seductress of the sheriff's son."

His eyes twinkled. "You certainly fit the role." He waggled his eyebrows at her. "Damn it, Edie, one look at you and I was in your thrall. Under your spell. There's something about a woman in cammies..."

She laughed so hard then that two saleswomen came to look and tears ran down her cheeks. "No lace and satin for you, huh?"

"Uncle Sam raised me. I lose it over cammies." He paused and winked. "Of course if you want to try the lace and satin I'd be happy to advise."

He kept his voice low so he couldn't be overheard, and she was grateful, but her heart skipped at least three beats at the suggestion. Lace and satin? Boy, would she love to try that sometime. The thought surprised her, as she'd never felt such a desire before, but then she remembered the baby bump. Wouldn't that look cute in some sexy getup? Her laughter renewed, but when he questioned her, she refused to explain.

Instead she turned her attention to the clothes. It wasn't as hard to face today for some reason. Maybe she'd crossed another hurdle in her adjustment. Seth offered no advice or opinion except that since it was getting cooler, she might want some long sleeves, maybe some flannel.

She settled on some jeans, some cotton flannel work shirts, and broke down for one prettier top in royal blue with some ridiculous sequins around the neck. She saw the way Seth's eyes smiled when she picked it, and wished she knew what he was thinking. She shooed him away though when she chose some underwear. It seemed ridiculous even to her after the intimacy they had shared, but she sent him on his way with the things she had already purchased.

"I'll meet you at the register. Now scat."

He laughed and did as told. And that's where she really lost her mind. Maybe the women around here worked hard and didn't want a lot of froufrou, but that evidently didn't extend to underwear. Feeling almost guilty, she selected some satin items and a couple of bras with a little lace. For the life of her, she couldn't have said why.

When she returned to the register, she sent him away while she paid. She didn't want him to see her selections. Not yet, anyway.

Where the heck had that thought come from? For an instant she almost returned the frilly items, then steeled herself and bought them. She could always find a trash can if she changed her mind.

Seth took most of the sacks from her when she joined him out front. "Lunch?" he asked. "We've got a great selection: Maude's, Maude's or Maude's."

"Lead me to a salad and a small sandwich."

"Big salad, but small sandwich not likely. We can take the leftovers home. And maybe I need to learn how to cook. When you see Maude's menu, the baby will probably gag, but dang, it's good food."

Maude was an experience all by herself. Edie wouldn't have thought that a woman so rude could manage to run a successful business, but there was no mistaking the success of it. The place was jammed and they got the last booth.

She sensed dozens of eyes on her, could almost feel the questions beating on the back of her head. Well, let them wonder. She focused her attention on Seth, which was surprisingly easy to do, and on the huge salad that came loaded with grilled chicken and a grumble from Maude about "expecting women need protein."

She almost choked.

Seth shrugged. "Told you," he said. "Judging by that salad, I get the role of villain. I hope she doesn't burn my steak."

"Would she?"

"Absolutely." He flashed a smile. "You never have to wonder where you stand with Maude or her daughters."

"I actually don't mind that."

"Most of us don't. She can take some getting used to, though."

Thirty seconds after he made that comment, Maude put a tall glass of milk in front of Edie. Evidently she wasn't going to get the coffee she had asked for. Her lips started twitching and she had to fight down a laugh.

When had laughing become so easy? Why was she feeling so light today, especially after a night of tossing and turning? She decided not to question it, however. She was sure all the worries would return in good time.

Seth kept the conversation light and general, sort of like the fun they'd had that night in Afghanistan, both of them seeking a break from reality. They kept it up all the way back to his house and the good feeling followed them right through the door.

He took her bags to the bedroom, saying, "Time to put the feet up, my lady. I think I'm going to go out and buy a bed for one of the spare rooms, so you might as well rest. I'll be back soon."

She wondered if he wanted to get away from her. Something must have shown on her face, though, because he reached out suddenly and gripped her upper arm gently. "You can come if you want. I just thought you might need a nap."

"I do," she admitted. The nearly sleepless night seemed to be catching up with her.

"I won't be long," he promised. "Just a bed they'll probably deliver tomorrow. You can even help me pick out the sheets in the morning if you want."

She smiled then, feeling better.

"And I swear," he added as he headed for the door, "I'm going to figure out something I can cook tonight."

"What are you going to cook in?"

"I bet if I tell my mom I'm in the mood to get domesticated, she'll have some pots to spare. I *do* have dishes, you know."

A smile tugged at the corners of her mouth. "Have you ever thought about how utterly capable you and I are with some things, and how utterly incapable we are with others?"

"Often lately," he admitted, looking rueful. "I've been staggering my learning curve, but it looks like I need to speed some of it up."

After Seth left, Edie debated whether to go nap in bed or on the recliner. She settled on the recliner after only a few minutes' thought. It seemed better somehow. Certain habits of safety hadn't departed, she realized. She wanted to know if anyone came into the house.

Life lived on the edge for too long, she thought as drowsiness began to sweep through her. Too long. When had she last truly relaxed?

With Seth that one night. And again today. Wondering about that, she fell into a deep sleep.

Chapter Seven

Seth had been using a twin bed as a convenience until he finished the renovations. So, of course, given all that was going on, did he just go buy another cheap one for one of the other bedrooms? Definitely not. He'd intended to get a king-size bed eventually, to fit his height better, and that's what he bought.

Try explaining that one to Edie, he thought as he wrote the check for the mattress and frame. But it would be stupid to buy yet another bed he wouldn't be likely to use in the long run.

He arranged for afternoon delivery the next day, then skipped the sheer idiocy of calling his mother and bought a set of cookware and utensils that were recommended by the clerk. Enough to manage some simple cooking, he figured, and while he claimed to be unable, he'd been married twice. There were a number of things he had learned to cook during those two spells, and he was pretty sure he hadn't forgotten how.

On the way out the door, heading for the grocery next, he spied a display of stuffed animals. Completing his idiocy, he bought a big stuffed bear for Edie. He could always claim it was for the kid if it bothered her.

He'd been thinking hard since yesterday when she'd thrown out that sarcastic suggestion that they should just get married. His response hadn't changed. It looked to him like the best way to handle *all* the things they were going to have to deal with. Logical. Good planning. Mission-specific action.

Thing was, he was beginning to realize that while that might sound like a good reason, things weren't apt to be so easy in the doing. Why? Because he was still as attracted as hell to the woman, and the more time he spent with her, the better he liked her and the more he wanted her.

If she didn't feel the same, marriage could be a disaster, for him anyway. He'd meant what he said, though, and if she decided to give it a shot, he'd give it his best one.

But he didn't really want what he'd offered. He wasn't sure he wanted to risk marriage again. Both of his had ended so painfully, though in different ways, that he'd pretty much made up his mind never to do that again. When you could avoid that kind of pain, it only made sense to do so.

But this was a whole different equation, one that involved a baby. Every fiber of his being rebelled at the thought of letting that child grow up with an absentee father. No child should have to do that, and even though many did, *his* was not about to be among them as long as he had breath in his body.

As short a time as Edie had been here, he'd begun to see a change in her. He guessed she was starting to trust him a bit. Certainly the very determined, hard-edged pilot was lowering her defenses a bit, showing less resistance to the idea of him as a father to her child and even for a few minutes here and there letting him see she had a softer side.

That was good. It meant they could deal, and they were going to be dealing, one way or another, for decades to come. He'd seen enough with his own family to know you didn't raise a kid to eighteen or twenty-two and then quit being a parent. No, that never quit, and not always because it was habit. They'd been there for him after both his marriages. They'd been there for him every single time he'd needed something. Parenting was a lifetime commitment.

But Edie wasn't looking that far down the road. He honestly couldn't imagine the devils and demons she must have been dealing with, facing a pregnancy all alone in a career field where such things still weren't exactly accepted. Oh, if she hadn't been a pilot, it wouldn't have been as difficult, but given her career track, given where she had wanted to go, it must have been hell. In some respects, the military hadn't caught up with itself. It had broadened the role for women, then didn't seem to know what to do when women did what women did, other than let them resign.

Not that he objected to the option, because he didn't. Children mattered. But for someone like Edie... Oh, he could easily imagine the subtle pressure to get rid of the baby or resign. Yeah, he could envision it quite clearly.

She'd withstood all of that, though, which showed a lot of backbone because he was familiar with the kinds of pressure senior officers could bring to bear, all without crossing any lines of proper conduct. Then, once she'd worked most of it through in her own mind, making a great many sacrifices, she'd hauled herself out here to do what she considered the honorable thing, planning to turn right around and continue dealing with all of this on her own.

She was one admirable woman in a lot of ways.

But he had to admit he liked the softer side of her, too. Just as he'd loved their tumble in the hay in Afghanistan, he was discovering his admiration extended beyond her fantastic piloting skills and her sexiness to the whole way she approached life. Duty and honor first. Facing tough situations and dealing with them.

Yet he sensed all of this was taking a serious toll on her. Well, why wouldn't it? He was grateful she had let him hold her this morning, little enough on his part. She needed to know she could turn to at least someone, and if he was it, so much the better for all of them. It'd make him feel like less of an ass, it might give the baby a father who was around and it might lighten her burden.

Right now, he seriously wanted to lighten her burden.

But he also had to be sure of himself, and he wasn't sure about some things. He hadn't been kidding her when he told her he still had a hair trigger. Twenty years in special ops, often on dangerous, deniable and redacted missions, hadn't left him a standard model male. He was different in ways that might be extremely important when raising a child. A part of him had necessarily become hardened. Other parts tended toward authoritarian. He was used to being obeyed. He could deal with messiness and things blowing up in his face, but those weren't ordinary situations. He knew exactly what he was capable of, some of it stuff other people never had to deal with in an entire lifetime.

On the other hand, training, experience and the years had taught him an extraordinary amount of self-control. He could clamp down on his emotions faster than a rattlesnake could strike. Become an automaton. He wasn't sure that was a good thing in a situation like this.

Look at him. His hair trigger had caused him to get angry with her. He hadn't clamped down fast enough that time. He guessed it was all situational, and this was a whole new situation.

In fact the side of himself he was showing Edie was like wearing an unfamiliar suit: careful, compromising, reasonable. He was walking on eggshells and it wasn't comfortable or natural. Unlike his two wives, Edie had probably met enough SEALs in her job to have some idea of what lay beneath the surface, but most of the civilized stuff about him was a veneer. At his core rested a highly trained barbarian, one to be unleashed only when needed. But what if it slipped the leash?

Back to that whole control thing. Control was everything on a mission, and if you had to, you flipped the switch of your emotions. On and off like some kind of light.

What the hell kind of father would that make him?

He pulled into the parking lot at the grocery and dialed his cell, calling his dad on *his* cell, the only sure way he wouldn't get his mother. It was not Marge he needed to talk to.

"What's up?" Nate asked his son.

"I'm transitioning."

"Got it."

"So how the hell do you do it? How do you go from being what I've been to being a decent father?"

Nate was silent for a long time. Seth began to wonder if anyone had an answer to that. Finally… "I'm not sure there's any one way. We all have our devils to deal with. But when your oldest sister was born, I held her in my arms and knew one thing for sure."

"Which was?"

"That I had a new mission and was going to give it my all. It wasn't so different from other missions, where your buddies are more important than you are. Where getting them out safely is your primary concern. You have the skills, son. They just need some fine-tuning. You also have a couple of dads as examples. Play the part until it fits."

Play the part until it fits. As he walked into the grocery, Seth guessed that was what he was doing. Playing a part because he didn't want to lose a son. Amazing how important that had become, how central to his life in such a short amount of time.

But was that fair, to play a part? Maybe it would be to the kid until it became comfortable, but what about Edie?

Still unsettled, he forced his attention to shopping. When he got home, he put the teddy bear in a closet.

In the morning, he and Edie settled on some navy blue sheets for the bed and a few pillows. Well, he pretty much settled and she went along. He sensed in her once again the resistance to thinking herself part of his life for the long term. He was going to have to find a way around that.

Her eyes grew huge, though, as she realized he was buying king-size sheets. He even thought he saw a little apprehension in her expression.

"King-size?" she said as they hit the street again.

"Well, the twin bed is really too short for me. I was just putting off getting the king-size until later. It didn't strike me as especially useful to buy another twin bed I'll never want, at least not in the near future."

"Oh."

Was she relieved? He couldn't tell. The damn eggshells again. Looking at his purchase of a bed as...what? An intent to jump her bones? Hell, he wouldn't mind that at all, but he sure wasn't going to do it unless she invited it in some way.

But dang, if he'd wanted her that night in Afghanistan, he wanted her even more now. Continued exposure to her wasn't inoculating him. Far from it. With each passing hour she looked increasingly pretty and increasingly sexy. He'd blown it for them out there, making an assumption he should never have made about her experience, and he didn't want to blow it again.

"You don't talk much," she remarked. "What are you thinking about?"

Damn, he was getting tired of eggshells, so he just told her flat out, "I'm thinking how sexy you are, and wishing we'd met under different circumstances."

He heard her gasp, but didn't look at her.

"You wouldn't have even noticed me under other circumstances," she said finally.

"I don't know where you get an idea like that. I'd have noticed you under any circumstances. You may not have guys buzzing around you like bees, but that's because you have some pretty good off-limits signs on your perimeter. You even tried to get rid of me when I came over to talk to you. Unfortunately for you, I don't heed those signs. I take them as a challenge."

They walked another half block in silence.

"You saw me as a challenge?"

He didn't know if he liked her tone of voice, but he took it on anyway. "To a point, yeah. But I'll tell you something, on my honor it would never have gone as far as it did except I saw the signs come down that morning when we woke. I never intended to take advantage of you."

He looked at her, saw her cheeks color faintly, but from the side he couldn't tell if it was anger or embarrassment.

"Am I still a challenge?"

"You're carrying my son inside of you. How could you not be a challenge? But you're still sexy as hell."

She swore quietly.

"Sorry," he said. "If you don't like peeks inside my head, don't ask."

She faced him then. "You know, Seth Hardin, you're driving me nuts. We can't have a discussion like this on a public street."

He pointed. "Half a block that way."

She started marching quick time, looking for all the world as if she were on parade, back stiff, strides even and firm. He kept up without difficulty.

"Don't get breathless," he said.

"Oh, shut up."

He almost grinned. No more eggshells, at least for now. The gloves were off.

She could barely stand still while he unlocked the front door. As soon as it closed behind him, she faced him, her hands clenched. "How dare you make this about us? This is supposed to be about the baby. That's it."

"Oh, no, lady, it's about us, too." He pointed at her belly, which still hardly showed. "That kid we made makes it about us."

"Only if you insist."

"Oh, I insist."

She glared at him. "You freaking SEALs have the world's biggest egos! Everything is about you."

"I didn't say this was about me, I said it was about *us*."

Her fists clenched even tighter. "You said it was about you when you said I was sexy. That's off the table."

"Sure, if you want."

"Big talk about a marriage of convenience," she spat. "Just friends. Hah! You just want to get into my pants again."

"Yes," he said frankly, "I do. But I won't as long as those signs are up. Believe it or not, I've always understood that no means no. But you're just going to have to live with the fact that I want you. Once will never be enough for me. Now I can put it on ice, if that's the way you want it, but you might as well know. I'm going to have evil, wicked, salacious thoughts about you at times. Damn it, I'm a man. What is it? Six times a minute?"

"Oh, hell." She threw up a hand. "Here I thought we were working toward some kind of agreement, so of course you throw a wrench in the works."

"I hate to tell you, but the wrench is already there. Two of them, actually. And you get to set the limits because there's a baby hostage here."

"Hostage?" She almost shouted the word. "Is that what you think I'm doing?"

"Aren't you, in a way? First you insist you want nothing from me. Then you keep threatening to leave when you don't like something. Okay, you haven't threatened that yet today, but I suspect you'll be doing it in a minute or two after this round. So I told you you're sexy. Most women would be flattered. They wouldn't be yelling at me about some rule I haven't broken yet."

"We haven't even established any rules yet. What are you talking about?"

"*We* might not have made any, but I keep running into

them when I talk to you. You've got all kinds of rules in your mind. How much Seth can do. How much Seth can be a father. You expect things of me and I don't even know what they are. And hanging over all this is a baby I intend to be a father to no matter what it takes. Now we can make this all-out war, or we can start talking about some of the important stuff, like how you and I are going to build a life *together* that will work for this child."

"Sex isn't part of that!"

He stepped closer. "Really?" he asked softly. "*Really?* Because I've seen how you look at me sometimes. You feel it, too."

"You can't build a relationship on that."

"But you can start one."

He fully expected her to stomp away, go pack her duffel and try to leave. That seemed to be the pattern. And he'd be here right by the door to stand in her way. Argue with her. Because he was getting to the point where *something* had to be settled, even if it was only that he'd be a weekend father, visiting once a month. *Something.* A starting point, instead of all this edging around.

But she didn't run. Instead her face twisted a bit and her hand flew to her belly. "Seth?" she gasped.

He didn't ask any questions. He shoved his hand in his pocket to verify that he had his keys, picked her up and swept her to his car to head to the hospital. He didn't even lock up behind them.

The next couple of hours proved to be among the longest in his life. Edie had her wallet on her, so he was able to fill out all the paperwork, but they wouldn't let him near her. Not family.

No, but one of the patients was family. He argued that

and got nowhere, of course. He didn't call anyone, but word seeped out anyway. Soon there was a gathering of the Tate clan, those still in town, except for Mary, who was on duty elsewhere in the hospital. That didn't prevent her husband, a doctor, from coming down, though, and it was from him that Seth finally got a modicum of information.

"There's nothing wrong. Nothing," David told him. "They're checking her thoroughly, but the baby is fine, the pregnancy is stable. You'll have to wait until they get the lab work back, though."

"I want to see her."

David shook his head. "Not right now. Soon. I'll make sure you get in there soon."

He ignored his parents and Wendy, pacing tight circles around the waiting room, mentally kicking himself in the butt repeatedly. He shouldn't have argued with her. The fight must have caused some kind of problem. What would he know?

"Seth, sit down," Marge implored finally. "I'm getting dizzy watching you, and it's not helping anything."

He dropped into a chair beside his mother. "We were having a fight. A disagreement. Suddenly she grabbed her stomach. Could a fight cause a problem?"

Marge took his hand. "No. When I was pregnant I tended to get irritable sometimes. Your dad and I had some real toe-to-toes. A pregnant woman isn't fragile unless there's a problem, and they'd have most likely noticed that by now."

He took what comfort he could from that, and the fact that David had said nothing appeared to be wrong with the pregnancy. But something was wrong, and it gnawed at him.

He shouldn't have fought with her. His own need to start clearing the air between them should not have driven him to that. But damn it, he *did* feel as if there were a hostage in this situation. Maybe she wasn't using the baby that way, but maybe it was *him* being held hostage.

God, he should have just shut his yap. He'd promised her time and space and then had come on like gangbusters. He needed a good knock in the head to drive sense into him.

This was a foreign situation. His usual methods of dealing with challenges were clearly the wrong ones. Bulling into a fight because you felt you needed to make some things clearer might work with one of his team members, but Edie wasn't one of them. He knew she was a capable, fearless pilot, a career woman, strong and determined, but he knew absolutely nothing about whether getting into an argument was something she avoided or something she was willing to do. Not really. Not yet.

And that was the whole damn problem.

"Seth?"

He looked up. David stood there. "Edie wants you."

Well, thank God for that. Maybe she didn't hate him yet. Or maybe she just wanted to tell him she never wanted to lay eyes on him again. God, he needed to learn to pussyfoot better.

But he still didn't pussyfoot. He walked into the cubicle. Her eyes opened and found him standing just inside the curtain. "So," he said, "am I about to be banished forever?"

"What?" Her eyes widened.

"I was an ass. A bull. An idiot."

To his amazement, she sighed, then smiled faintly.

"Everything's fine. It was probably a gas bubble, or the baby kicking the wrong place. I'm fine."

"You still didn't answer me."

She stared at him. "Well, unless you have a problem with the idea, would you please take me home?"

His heart skittered uncomfortably. "Home. Which home?"

"Your place."

He kicked into high gear as the weight lifted. "Absolutely. Do you want some help dressing?"

Her smile broadened a shade. "You'd love that, wouldn't you?"

"Probably," he admitted. "I'd sure like to help somehow."

"You're taking me home. The dressing part I can do myself as soon as they take this IV out of my hand."

He stepped closer and took her hand, the one that didn't have a needle in it. "I'm sorry."

"Don't be. While I've been lying here scared to death, I thought about some of the things you said. So here's my new rule."

"What's that?"

"No hostage taking."

"I shouldn't have..."

She interrupted. "I had time to think about this from a perspective other than my own. I haven't been fair or just about this. It's time to start. We'll talk more once they let me go."

Before he could say another word, a nurse shooed him out and he was standing in the hallway outside, waiting.

He felt sappy happy for the first time in years. He was getting another chance.

* * *

Edie was astonished to find Nate, Marge and Wendy all there. As they accompanied her and Seth out to the car, she couldn't help but think it would be nice to have a family like this, one that was there immediately in times of difficulty. She'd never had that, not like this. Inevitably, the notion wormed into her mind that this would be good for her son, very good. Far better than what she could provide alone.

Marge announced she was bringing over a casserole for them later. Wendy said they'd postpone their dinner plans for a few days but made Seth promise to give Edie her cell number just in case.

In short, she felt wrapped in love and concern, something she had never dreamed might happen. She was a stranger, but she'd been pulled into their tight circle so quickly it amazed her.

On the way back to the house, a random thought occurred to her. "You missed the bed delivery."

"Like hell. There's one thing about having family. Yuma's over there to take care of it. I hope he hasn't already left. I think you'd like him a whole lot."

"I suspect I will. I still can't believe your brother-in-law David came racing down to the E.R. to manage things."

"That's the way this family works. Hell, most of the time it's the way this county works, from what I've seen. I'm not completely clued in yet, because I've only been here when I had leave, but folks around here are pretty good about not ignoring a neighbor in trouble. Mom's casserole won't be the last one," he warned her.

"But I'm not sick."

"They won't care. You had a scare. Hell, so did I."

"I'm sorry."

"For what? You had a sharp pain, and seeing as how neither of us are pros at pregnancy, we did the smart thing. I was going crazy, though, not being allowed to see you. Not family. I'm sure David violated a whole bunch of rules when he finally told me you were okay."

"Oh." She fell silent, thinking about that. Another thing she hadn't considered. The thought of him being kept away if something happened with their baby, now or later, seriously troubled her.

When they got back to the house, Yuma was still there. A good-looking man, Edie thought, even though he appeared to be nearly twenty years older than Wendy.

"Bed's in place, like you wanted," he told Seth after introductions were made. Then he focused his attention on Edie. "Wendy says you'd like to take the stick on one of our Hueys."

"I'd love it."

He gave her a slow smile. "Then count on it. I'll ride in the right-hand seat, but you've flown one before, haven't you?"

"In training."

"Great. Then you're going to have a blast, especially around the mountains. But given where you've been flying, I guess you know that. Okay, I'm off." He patted the pager on his belt. "Believe it or not, I'm on call."

"Why wouldn't I believe it?" Seth asked humorously. "You and Wendy are almost always on call."

"Few hands, much work. Nice meeting you, Edie. I'm looking forward to flying with you."

Then he was gone.

Seth guided Edie back to the recliner. "Okay, now to business."

"What business?"

"What were your discharge orders?"

She reached into her pocket and pulled out a folded piece of paper. "No big deal."

Seth scanned them. "Take it very easy for twenty-four hours. That's not so bad."

"Except that I'm not built to be a couch potato."

He chuckled quietly. "You can tolerate one day."

But she could see tension around his eyes and once again wondered what was going on inside him. Was she ready to risk asking? Look what had happened earlier. His thoughts seemed to run in very different directions than hers.

Or maybe she was just deluding herself. Maybe they weren't as far apart as she wanted to pretend. She settled onto the recliner with a sigh and elevated her feet. At once Seth started unlacing her boots.

"We've got to get you something more reasonable to wear around the house. Desert boots are overdoing it, don't you think?"

She cocked a brow at him. "Have you ever found anything more comfortable?"

"Well, no, but certainly lighter."

He didn't stop with removing her boots, but sat at the foot of the chair and began to massage her ankles and feet. He didn't ask if she minded, and she certainly didn't. With each gentle knead, relaxation seemed to pour through her.

"Boy, that feels good," she said finally and looked into his smiling eyes.

"That was my hope. A foot massage is at the top of my list for causing relaxation. It's amazing how rubbing the feet can ease knots everywhere. I had a high school coach once who recommended walking barefoot on grass to achieve the same thing."

"It's been a long time since I thought of doing anything barefoot."

His smile faded a shade. "I know. You get so that if you pull those boots off, they'd better be in arm's reach."

"You'd know better than anyone." She waited, wondering what he might share, understanding that he'd never be able to really talk about the things he'd done as a SEAL. That would forever be a silent chapter. When he didn't immediately answer, she let her eyes close and gave herself up to the wonder of having her feet rubbed for the first time in her life. Heaven!

All of a sudden, a ridiculous thought popped out of her mouth. "Do they redact your memories, too?"

His hands stilled, then he said, "I wish." He laughed quietly, though. "I don't have to tell you. We learn to live with it all, don't we?"

"I suppose. I can occasionally wake up with a nightmare about having a close call, but I'm glad it doesn't happen often. A sound that reminds me of rotors can flash me back in an instant. I hear the bird, I smell it, taste the metal and fuel and exhaust in the air. But just for an instant."

"I don't flash back much. I don't know why I'm so damn lucky. Maybe because it got to be so routine after so many years. Danged if I know. Or maybe something in me just quit. We did what we had to do. Unfortunately, too many of us struggle with it for years."

"I know," she answered quietly. "So we're lucky."

"I guess so." He smiled, an expression that caused her insides to melt and a tingle to begin between her thighs. She wanted to tamp down on it then wondered why. He'd already expressed that he found her sexy, and despite her initial reaction, she liked knowing that. Anyway, there were her discharge orders protecting her. Take it easy for a whole day. She doubted wild lovemaking, such as they'd shared that one night, qualified as taking it easy.

"Is he moving?" Seth asked.

She realized her hand had come to rest on her belly again. "Yeah. Sometimes I wonder if he ever sleeps."

"What does it feel like to you?"

"Mostly gentle little pokes, sometimes almost like small moving gas bubbles. It depends on how force-ful he's being, but the feeling gets stronger with time."

"Not painful?"

"Nope. Well, maybe not until today. It could have been a digestion problem. They said that's common in pregnancy."

"I guess I need to get a book and read up. Have you thought about names?"

Her breath stopped, just briefly. "No." But a volcano of realization erupted in her at the thought. All this time she told herself she'd been coping. All this time she thought she had accepted the reality of this baby. After all, she could feel it moving within her, and that was as real as it got.

But she suddenly understood she'd been keeping up some kind of pretense with herself. Maybe a wall. Right up until the last few days, she'd been objectifying this baby, calling it "it," "the kid," "the baby." The closest she'd come to thinking of it as a real child had been when she referred to him as "Junior." Hell, she had only re-cently gotten to thinking of it as a him.

Seth already referred to "my son" and "my baby." He had taken possession. She had not. In some way she had refused, all the while planning everything out, to own her own child in some deeply emotional way.

"Edie? Did I say something wrong?"

She had to force herself to look at him as a tide of guilt overwhelmed her. She was soon to be a mother but had been thinking of her child in such a detached way. Distancing herself.

"I'm going to be a lousy mother."

Surprise dashed across his face. "What brought that on?"

"A good hard look inward." She hesitated, wondering if she should even try to explain this to him. She looked away again, dealing with the storm inside herself. She didn't like what she was seeing. Objectifying this child. What kind of mother did that?

"Edie?" The prompt was quiet, gentle.

Just another assignment. Just another problem to be dealt with. Not a living human being who would soon be utterly dependent on her caring and love. She hadn't given that love yet, had in fact avoided it. Had she been stupid enough to think that could continue, especially after the baby was born?

Seth stopped rubbing her feet and moved until he was kneeling beside the chair. With his fingertips, he turned her face toward him. "Talk to me," he insisted quietly. "We've both got a lot to work through. It's amazing how helpful talking can be."

"You don't do much of it."

"I do more than you in some ways. I have this tight little self-protective core and I know it. Twenty years in special ops makes it essential. Well, I get the feeling you have one, too. I respect that. But maybe we need to edge out of them a bit, cross those barriers. We'd have to do it with our baby."

"That's just it," she admitted finally. She closed her eyes because she didn't want to see his reaction. "I just realized I've been objectifying this baby. Making it something other than my child. Oh, it's my responsibility, but thinking of it as *my* child, *my* son...I've been avoiding it. Until I got here I didn't even think of him as a he. Just as *the kid*. He could have been anyone's kid, the way I was thinking." She paused. "Maybe I didn't always talk that way, but that's how I was thinking. Trying not to feel."

He spoke slowly, as if feeling his way. "Is that a crime?"

Her eyes snapped open. "What if I keep doing that?"

"Somehow I think you won't be able to keep on doing it once you hold our baby. I just don't read you that way. You've got nerves of steel when you need them, but people go into CSAR out of passion. You've got a lot of passion to get where you've gotten. You give a damn about things, and you're going to give a damn about this baby in time."

"So sure?"

One corner of his mouth lifted. "Absolutely. Once we sort out all the things that have been worrying you and bugging you, you'll have room for the rest of it. You've had a lot to deal with, Edie, and you've been pretty much handling it solo. Of course you went into mission mindset. But once a lot of this gets ironed out, you'll have the emotional space to think about actually being a mom."

"I just don't know how to cross over."

"I asked my dad about that."

"You did?" Her eyes widened a bit.

"Of course I did. I know what I am, who I've become. I probably know better than most people because I've had to get into the dark places most people never have to find in themselves. So I asked my dad how he made the transition. How he crossed back over the lines you have to cross in special ops. How you transition from being a warrior to a dad."

"What did he say?"

"Once you hold that baby for the first time, it becomes the center of everything, basically. So I think you'll do it, whether you figure it out or not in advance. You've pretty much been in a defensive crouch for months. Defending yourself, defending your decisions, trying to defend your career and, yes, even defending your decision to keep this baby. Well, you can relax a little now. I'll take on as much as I can, as much as you'll let me."

He made it sound so easy. She resisted, then realized that maybe it was just that easy. Anything she didn't figure out now, she would figure out later. "I've been thinking about a lot of things, but not about the actuality," she admitted. "Don't most people by this point start buying baby clothes or something?"

"You're asking the wrong person about that."

Despite a feeling of disappointment with herself, she felt the corners of her mouth lift a little. "I haven't even wanted to face maternity clothes."

"You faced them pretty good yesterday."

"I guess." At least she hadn't choked. "The other thing is…" She hesitated.

"Yes?" He waited.

"After what you said about not being allowed to find out what was going on with me because we're not family…it struck me how awful it would be if the baby had a problem and you were cut out like that."

"Or if *you* have a problem," he reminded her quietly.

"I know a lot of people are forced to deal with that, but there's got to be some way around it. It just hit me hard that it would be so unfair to you. You've already committed to raising this child. That means you're bound to get involved and care."

"I already care," he admitted. "And it's our child. Our son."

"Our son," she repeated. The words came more easily now. "What if he got sick? What if something happened to both of us and you couldn't do a damn thing except pace a waiting room like you did today? That's awful. I don't want that to ever happen. And what if, God forbid, something should happen to me? You've got to have a right to this…our son. I'd hate to think of anything else."

His next words surprised her. "Thank you."

"For what?"

"For telling me that you're ready to let me be part of our child's life. However we work it out, that's what I needed to hear."

He actually smiled at her. She had the worst urge to reach out a hand and touch him, run her fingers over his hair, cup his cheek. She still wanted him in the same way she had wanted him that night months ago. Maybe even more now. She stopped herself, though. Too much remained unsettled to confuse them even more by having sex.

"You're accepting this faster than I am," she remarked.

"Well, I've had a whole lot less adjusting to do. I'm going to be a father. Awesome. No career to bollix things up, no superior officers making suggestions they shouldn't make, none of it. I got the easy end."

"That remains to be seen," she said, feeling an errant bubble of humor. "You can take the middle-of-the-night feedings."

He laughed, and the sound melted something inside her. He didn't press her, though, didn't seem to take it as a statement of fact, but as a joke. Which is how she meant it. For now. She still wasn't sure she wanted him around all the time. But she was rapidly coming to the conclusion she wanted him around at least some of the time.

"Okay," he said presently, "let me throw a couple of things out here. No pressure. No need to make up your mind right now. We can solve a lot of these problems by going to an attorney. Probably cost an arm and a leg, but we can get legal papers, I'm sure, acknowledging my paternity, giving me medical power of some kind… I mean, I'm sure a lawyer could sew things up so you wouldn't have to worry about those things."

"Probably. Have you got an arm and a leg?"

He waved one arm with a wink. "I can manage."

"And the other thing?" Although she already knew, for some reason she wanted to hear him say it again.

"You know. Marriage. That's an automatic slam dunk on legal issues. We can work out the details of how to manage it between us, but it's a valid option."

She nodded but didn't answer. The option was still there, and it was sinking deeper and deeper ever since they had first discussed it. Then she asked, "Seth, what if it blows up?"

"I've survived one ugly divorce. I can survive another. Except I want one promise—that it won't be ugly. That wouldn't be good for our son. If you decide you can't stand the sight of me, just tell me to pack. I don't need the whole vituperation thing."

"I don't do much vituperation."

"Good." There was no smile in his eyes now, but rather a steely look. She wondered if he was remembering, or assuming a mantle of determination. Either way, for a few seconds he looked harder than a diamond-edged blade.

"After what you've been through, I'm surprised you can even suggest marriage."

A smile didn't quite reach his eyes. "Ah, it wasn't all bad. Trust me. It was just hell when they ended. Our son is a good enough reason for me to give it another shot. Your rules, of course. But the boy is a good enough reason for me. The question is whether he is for you."

Chapter Eight

Several nights later, Seth left the house in the wee hours to take a walk. Edie slept in the king-size bed in his room, over her objections that he needed the extra space. She'd subsided when he'd explained that he was sure the room was mold- and mildew-free, something he couldn't say with absolute certainty about the other bedrooms.

Not exactly true, but true enough that he didn't feel he was lying. He wanted her to have the more comfortable bed.

He wanted his son to have the best. His son. The idea had settled into his heart in a way that still surprised him. It was a warm feeling, and wonderful sense of anticipation, and it thawed some of the places he'd had to put in ice over the years. Nor did that thawing trouble him. It made him feel surprisingly good, actually.

Not another word about how they were going to deal with the legalities of this, but he got the sense she was trying him on for size anyway. They had done some remodeling stuff together, things he was sure wouldn't cause her a risk, like reframing a wall with arsenic-free wood. He'd done all his sawing outside but she had followed anyway, accepting the dust mask he'd pointedly handed her.

She didn't mind carrying boards, she loved using the

nail gun and she'd even proved adept at helping him with some of the wiring.

Then there were their forays into cooking. Those had turned into a great deal of fun with a lot of laughter. They discovered they were messy cooks, and she had joked that she couldn't even boil water, but they'd managed to put together some decent meals, despite an almost daily flow of casseroles from people around town, most of which filled the freezer. Of course he'd phoned Marge a time or two, but she was more than willing to advise. The only problem he had was keeping her from coming over to do it for them.

God bless his mother, he thought. It must be killing her to stay away, but Seth had this feeling that he and Edie were at a fragile point, and he didn't want anything knocking this slowly growing understanding off-kilter.

Edie insisted on doing the laundry for both of them, so he did all the sweeping and vacuuming. Not that he wouldn't have done it all if she weren't there.

Trying it on. That's what it felt like, except it would be different when she went back to her job. Then he'd be the househusband, he guessed, if she decided she wanted him around.

The thought caused him to yank himself back. He was in danger of envisioning something that might never happen. He did crack a grin, though, at the thought of greeting Edie when she came home with a kid on his hip and an apron around his waist. Damn, wouldn't his old buddies have a field day with that?

It was certainly a new way of thinking for him. SEALs were the ultimate in machismo. It oozed out of them and they were proud of it. A man's world, for men only. Never mind that he'd seen more than one turn into putty at the hands of their own kids, at least temporarily.

But he didn't have to fit that culture anymore, and he was actually enjoying the wind-down as it occurred. Little by little he was growing comfortable in his skin in a new way, finding parts of himself he'd never really had much time for before.

So this whole dad thing was easier on him than the mom thing was on Edie. That was as plain as the nose on his face. The only way he could figure out how to make any of this easier for her was to step in wherever she might let him and relieve her of some of the burden.

He somehow suspected that notion was really chapping at her. She was as fiercely independent as anyone he'd ever worked with. In fact, she had her own form of machismo.

Thinking about it that way gave him a better feel for how to navigate these shoals. Assuming, of course, that he wasn't wrong. The woman had been through a private hell these past months and was still trying to be tough and hold the reins.

He admired that more than he'd probably ever be able to let her know. In a way, they were both very much alike. He supposed he needed to find a way to get that similarity through. It might make the rough ground a little smoother.

But two very strong-willed people shackled together for the sake of a baby? He couldn't blame her for her doubts. Maybe he should be having more of his own.

But under no circumstances was he going to pretend his son didn't exist.

As he approached the house, he saw that the kitchen light was on. Edie was up. Hoping nothing was wrong, he started running. His body enjoyed opening up, enjoying the exercise, but his mind wasn't remotely happy about the possible reasons for it.

He never locked up when he got the urge for a nighttime ramble, but with Edie sleeping upstairs, he had. He fumbled for his keys, struggling to get them into the lock in the dark—he hadn't turned on the porch light—and finally burst into the house.

"Edie?"

"In the kitchen."

Well, she sounded all right. So he paused to close the door and slowed his pace as he went to her. She was leaning against the counter, wrapped in a blue terry-cloth robe, cradling a mug of coffee in her hands.

"Something wrong?" he asked.

"Not a thing. I heard you go out and then I couldn't get back to sleep. Do you go out at night a lot?"

"Once in a while. I like it out there."

"You probably did an awful lot of things at night."

He couldn't deny it. "It's peaceful out there," he answered, evading the question. If it had even been a question. "Everything's so quiet except for the breeze, and when I can see through the canopy of trees, the stars are beautiful."

She smiled faintly. "Grab some coffee, or do you want to go back to sleep?"

The adrenaline jolt he'd gotten from seeing the light on had eliminated any possibility of sleep.

"Why don't we get comfortable in the living room?" he suggested. "I can even pull out some of those rolls we bought if you're hungry."

"I seem to be always hungry." She turned, freshening her coffee, then headed for the living room.

Taking that as a yes, he found the package of cheese Danish and sliced some up onto plates for them. Juggling two plates and his own cup of coffee, he joined her.

She thanked him when he put one plate on the end table beside her. Then he retreated to his own chair, facing her.

"Any idea why you couldn't get back to sleep?" he asked, noting that she once again rested her hand over her stomach. He'd realized some time ago that that seemed to be instinctive in pregnant women, but he wondered if it was a physical cue to the direction of her thoughts. They'd kind of put things on hold since after her hospital visit, and he had no idea what she was thinking about the huge questions facing them. Nor did he feel inclined to press her. She'd talk when she was ready.

If his job had taught him one thing, it was that there were times when patience was essential.

She ate a few bites of pastry, then licked her fingers and let her head fall back.

"You have a life and family here," she remarked.

Instantly, his focus on her tightened. He waited, letting her lead.

"You must want to stay here," she said.

Ah. "Well, this is the first time I've stayed here longer than my leave. I haven't exactly put down deep roots. Sometimes I wonder if I can."

Her blue eyes settled on him. "Really? With all this family, I would have thought it would be easy."

"I'm basically a gypsy," he admitted with a shrug. "Too many years of not knowing where my boots would be next week or next month. Always on the move. Probably about the same for you."

"I always had a base."

"So did I. Not the same thing."

"I guess not." She closed her eyes briefly then looked at him again. "The future's all cloudy right now. But I keep worrying anyway, probably about a lot of things that aren't in my control. I can't resign. The air force is all I know. Flying helicopters is all I know, and anyway, I love it. But even without helos, what would I do? I'm not sure I'd like anything else anywhere near as much. So any way I stack it up, I'm likely to raise a rootless baby." She hesitated. "I'm not sure that's a good thing."

"Who can be? But the love moves with you, right?"

"That's the theory." She gave a long sigh. "But that's not the sum anyway, and I keep gnawing the same problems over and over and getting nowhere, really. Maybe I'm just worrying too damn much."

"Maybe. I can't say. I'm in a better position than you. I've retired. I can do whatever I damn well please now, and whatever we decide is best for our son. You have a whole lot of other things to deal with."

"Does it bother you?" she asked suddenly, "Don't you miss it? All that action and adrenaline?"

"Sometimes," he admitted. "And there was an undeniable sense of purpose to it that I've been missing, but my body wasn't up to it anymore. I didn't want to be the weak link. And I didn't want a desk job. That would drive me nuts."

"So the decision wasn't easy?"

"Hell no. Took me a couple of years to settle on it. I know I'd promised Maria that I'd take a hike at twenty years, but once she was gone…" He shrugged a shoulder. "It wasn't easy. But it was right."

"I've been living alone a long time. I'm still not sure how I'd adapt to sharing space all the time."

He waited, tension growing in him as he wondered where she was heading.

"But this time with you has been easy. You're not difficult to get along with, usually."

"My training," he answered simply. "I worked with a team, often in very close quarters. You learn not to step on other people's toes pretty quickly."

"I guess."

"You have the same skills."

"I'm not sure about that. When I was off duty, I had the Bachelor Officers' Quarters. Have I been driving you nuts?"

"Not a bit. Not one little bit. Of course, I suspect most of you is still packed in your duffel. Where are you going with this?"

She eyed him and sighed. "Marriage. You hold it out like it's a perfect answer. Maybe it is, or at least as perfect as one can be in this situation, but it remains, I don't know if I can live with another person. And what if we chafe each other with time? How do we deal with that?"

"By behaving like adults. Like colleagues. Look, I've been married. I was sure as hell head over heels in love with Maria, and when she died I didn't want to live. They even took me off active operations for a while until they were positive I wouldn't do something stupid."

Her entire face seemed to droop. "I'm so sorry, Seth."

"Thanks." He shrugged away the melancholy that tried to rise in him. "Anyway, I had a point to that. I was crazy in love with that woman, but that didn't mean it was always easy. No relationship, whatever kind, is always easy. The question is whether you deal with the problems or throw your hands up, or do something one of you will regret. The question is, can we be reasonable adults?"

One corner of her mouth quirked up. "I've never met anyone who is reasonable all the time, no matter how adult."

"True," he admitted. "I'm not saying we'll never have a spat. That's human nature. It's what we do about it, it's the places we choose not to go when we have one, that matter."

She ate another mouthful of Danish, took another sip of coffee, then leaned back a little, holding her mug in both hands, staring up at the ceiling. Thinking. He let her be.

It wasn't easy, considering the things that were roiling in him. The longer he was with her, the harder he knew any so-called marriage of convenience was going to be. He wanted her with every cell in his being, and for all his talk about how enduring relationships were built on other things, he knew damn well what a strain it was going to be for him to be constantly around Edie without ever making love to her.

He'd already tried it on for size, and desire was hammering at him more than he wanted to admit. Her scent, the sound of her voice, the sight of her smile, all of it carried him back to that one night, a huge reminder of a conflagration that he suspected might just have barely begun.

To live with her for years and never pursue the promise of that? He'd be a fool not to admit he'd be signing on for a tour in hell, at least in that regard. But he'd spent much of the past twenty years frequently visiting hell, and he supposed he could do it for another twenty, if that's how she wanted it. Because he was going to have a son.

That child loomed huge in his perspective. No sacrifice too great. A son. Beginning, middle and end to any and all arguments.

"I can do this by myself," she said.

He felt his stomach sink, but didn't argue. Her independence was at her very core, and that was one thing he would not argue with. "You can," he agreed, much as it pained him.

"But given the way I live..." She sighed. "If I had a routine job it would be different. If I wasn't looking at another eight or ten years of being bounced around like a ping-pong ball, I could do it."

He remained silent, letting her work it through, glad that she was talking more about it. At least he knew where she was on the field of play. Somewhat, anyway.

"Hell," she said, "I could do it anyway. I know I could. But I'm not sure it would be good for...our son. Not with only one parent."

He spoke carefully. "If there was no choice, I have no doubt you'd do an excellent job. But there's a choice now. A number of them, actually. Everything from leaving the boy with me when you have to be away, to us getting it together on a permanent basis."

"You did kind of open a can of worms with that," she said. He was relieved that she sounded wry, not angry.

Then her eyelids started to droop. He waited until he was sure she had dozed off, then rose, carefully removing the mug from her hands.

Damn, he thought as he walked softly into the kitchen, this woman was taking him on a whirlwind ride into utterly unknown territory. Both of his wives had been fascinating women to him, but Edie was in a class by herself when it came to complexity. And she really wanted a fully detailed mission plan, which, like all mission plans, was impossible. The unexpected always happened.

He returned to the living room to watch her sleep. She was so damn beautiful. He liked to look at her, and he liked her, just that simple. And she was carrying his child.

He smiled to himself. A better bomb couldn't have dropped into his life.

"Are you sure you aren't just looking for a new sense of purpose?"

Edie challenged him with the question over breakfast.

"If I am, I've already found it. Too late."

"Oh. Well, what if the baby didn't exist? What if it was just me?"

He put down his utensils and looked at her. "If it were just you, I'd have already carried you upstairs to my bed and done all the things with you I couldn't do that morning in Afghanistan. If it were just you, I'd be making love to you right now. I want you every bit as much as I did then, and even more now that I'm getting to know you."

Then he stood up and walked out.

Wow, she thought. Just wow. "That's no marriage of convenience," she called after him.

"Depends on the ground rules," he called back. Then she heard the front door close behind him.

She slapped her palm on the table, angry with herself, then put her face in her hands. Was she losing her mind? Why had she brought that up? It was ridiculous given that there was no way to change the facts.

No, she'd brought it up because she was beginning to realize she wanted him around, all right, but not just for the sake of the baby. Their *son*. She wanted more than that.

And apparently he was willing to give it to her, at least the sex part. But what about the rest? God, this was so messy sometimes she couldn't believe it.

Then a thought hit her so hard she almost felt punched. Nobody went into something like this, for whatever reason, knowing how it would all turn out. Nobody. She ought to know that. You could plan a mission down to the last detail and the unexpected still happened.

When it came to having a child, when it came to marriage, everyone was flying on hope. It was impossible to predict, impossible to tie up into neat little packages and be sure that absolutely nothing would happen to change anything.

Every time she climbed into the cockpit, she was being the ultimate optimist. Absolutely certain she wouldn't have a mechanical failure, or that if she did she could deal with it. Absolutely certain she wouldn't crash. Absolutely certain she'd evade gunfire and RPGs and all the rest of it. Absolutely certain she could come down on the lip of a mountain cliff and not bang her rotors into rocks.

But none of that was an absolute certainty, and on many of her missions, the odds hadn't been good at all.

But she forged ahead optimistically. Being cautious and careful insofar as she could, but taking huge risks at the same time in the confidence that she would handle them.

Was this so damn different?

Was all this constant worrying simply another way

of trying not to face the future? Like playing with puzzle pieces to try to figure out the picture without putting them together because then she'd have to see it, like it or not?

All her training hammered on preparedness. The air force devised every possible problem it could so its pilots would be prepared to deal with them, but even so the impossible and unexpected happened. She'd buried a few friends because of that. Cascade failures. RPGs. Miscalculations. Whole bunches of things could escape your control, so you just didn't think about them.

Well, this really wasn't so very different. It was time to take a risk. To move forward instead of hanging back because she wanted every detail planned out. Life just didn't allow that, no matter how hard you tried. It happened, often with unintended consequences, like the baby she carried inside of her.

What, after all, was the likelihood that she'd have sex just once in her life, with a man using a condom, and still get pregnant? Probably not very likely over the span of a lifetime, but over the span of one night, the odds had gone from 2 or 3 percent failure rate to 100 percent.

Yes, there were some things she had to be sure of, like the fact that she was going to keep this baby. Some idea of the changes she'd need to make to her career and lifestyle. But by and large it was going to remain a huge unknown until it happened. Whatever it was.

Just like going on a mission in enemy territory.

Except this probably wouldn't be nearly as deadly. It might prove painful, but not deadly.

"Crap," she said to the empty kitchen. Playing games with herself. Denial in so many forms a psychologist probably couldn't name them all.

Not very cute, not very smart. There was a cliff she needed to deal with, laden with risks, but it had to be climbed because in four months she was going to be a mother.

What she ought to be doing was counting herself lucky that her baby's father wanted to be part of all this. She wouldn't have blamed him for heading for the hills.

But that wasn't Seth, and there was a steadiness and constant determination in him that she had come to appreciate. She wanted that in her child's life. Maybe even in her own.

Forget love. Many years ago, she'd dreamed about it, but over the years she'd come to count it as a problem. How many marriages had she seen fail? Too many. How many friends had she nursed through breakups? Too many.

So maybe love wasn't the best reason for an undertaking like this. Maybe there were other reasons, better ones, as long as your expectations matched reality.

The idea of marriage still made her uncomfortable, but when she remembered how Seth had been cut out during her short hospital stay, she knew they were going to have to deal with that somehow. She knew how she would have felt in his shoes: frantic and furious.

The easy way or the expensive way, that had to be dealt with. She had to make arrangements so that if anything happened to her he would get their child.

As for her career...well, if he was willing to step in, that might get back on track.

But oddly, as she sat there in the morning light, she wondered if that was really what she wanted anymore.

Three days later, Seth drove her out to a small airport to fly the Huey with Yuma. Excitement was building in her, the itch to take the stick again and fly around in the air. She'd been grounded for months now, and she hated it. She missed flying. For her it was a deep-rooted passion, never just a job.

They met Yuma and Wendy in the small office of the emergency response unit. This morning it was just the two of them and a bored-looking young man who was evidently the dispatcher.

"Everybody else is resting up," Yuma said as he shook their hands. "We had a big pileup out on the state highway last night and had to fly three patients to a trauma center. I hope it's a quiet morning." He looked at Edie. "Wendy's coming with, in case we get a call." Then he turned to Seth. "You stay here, man. If we have to race to a scene, you'd be excess baggage."

"No problem," Seth said. "I didn't expect to go. I brought my own entertainment." He pulled a paperback from his hip pocket.

Wendy laughed. "You guys. Always prepared."

Yuma positioned Edie in the left hand seat, the pilot's seat, and refreshed her about the controls. "We can't stay out long, sorry to say. We have a tight fuel budget."

Edie hesitated. "Then maybe I shouldn't fly at all."

Yuma shook his head. "We have a certain allowance for training. I don't have to tell you we can't go too long without flying. Never wise."

"It's been a couple of months for me, and even longer since I took the stick in a Huey."

He flashed a smile. "I'm right here, Edie. You'll do fine."

At last she hit the ignition and listened to the rotors wind up, that unforgettable *whop-whop* that was so distinctive to Hueys. Her excitement mounted, and behind the microphone she felt a smile stretch her face until it couldn't get any wider. Flying again!

Takeoff was a breeze, but once she started flying forward, she wobbled a bit as she got used to the dynamics of the metal monster around her.

"Doing great," Yuma said in her earphone.

"Like a baby learning to walk all over again." She heard him laugh.

"I'm belted in," Wendy said from the rear. "Have at it."

It didn't take long. So much of flying was feel, and she got the feel for this bird quickly. "She's a solid girl," she said to Yuma.

"One of the best ever built," he agreed. "You ought to think about flying one more often."

"Not likely. I'll be teaching others how to fly Pave Hawks when I get back on status."

"I was talking about here."

Her hand jerked infinitesimally on the stick, and the helo juddered a tiny bit. "What are you talking about?"

"I want to cut back on my hours. We've been kicking the idea around for some time. I know you probably won't even consider it, but I'm just mentioning it. It's pretty much the same job you do right now, without any flak. I like the no-flak part."

He let the subject drop, and she, too, let go of it. It didn't fit. But damn, she was enjoying flying again. She headed them toward the mountains, laughed when they hit some turbulence, passed low over some trees, then sighed and headed back, talking to a rather lackadaisical tower control. Returning made her sad. She'd have loved to be up here for hours and really put the Huey through her paces.

But at last she hovered over the landing pad and set

them down. There was more of a bump than she was used to, but only because she wasn't accustomed to landing this bird.

It killed her to pull off the headset, killed her to listen to the rotors wind down. But at last she had to climb out and return to life on the ground.

That was when the exhilaration hit her. Standing on the pavement under the shadow of the slowly turning rotors, she threw out her arms, spun around and cried, "That was *great!*"

Wendy and Yuma both laughed. Wendy took her hand and Yuma patted her back. Seth emerged from the office and came toward her with a grin. "Great?" he asked.

"Absolutely great! God, I've missed that." She turned to Yuma and gave him an unexpected hug. "Thanks so much for that."

His smile turned crooked. "Hey, I was just a passenger."

They had just started making plans once again for the dinner that hadn't happened yet when a call came in. Time to transport a critical patient from the local hospital to a bigger medical center. Seth and Edie hung around to watch Wendy and Yuma take off, headed for the local hospital.

She didn't say a word to Seth about the suggestion Yuma had made. She still didn't know whether she even wanted to consider it.

"The ERT also does mountain rescue," Seth remarked as they walked to the car. "It's not all about emergency transport. We've got some good ground teams in this county."

"Are you thinking about it?"

"Along with being a deputy, it's crossed my mind. I have the training for it."

"You certainly do. In fact you could probably give the training."

He seemed to grow pensive as they headed back to his place, and she wondered what he was thinking. He'd already looked into the possibility of two jobs here, but he was prepared to throw that all up to follow her around the world. Damn, didn't that make her feel awful.

Yet, there was still their baby. Hadn't she already pondered a bit about how a child had to come first in everything?

Almost without realizing it, she muttered a cuss word under her breath, wondering why there seemed to be some new wrinkle at every turn. As soon as the word slipped past her lips, she hoped he'd missed it in the car noises. He hadn't.

"I thought you just had a great time. Why are you cussing?"

She could have offered almost any excuse under the sun, but it was growing increasingly clear to her that denial was dangerous, that concealing things was pointless. They had a lot to deal with, and ignoring any part of it could have bad consequences. Honesty, not evasion, had to be the policy from here on out.

"I was just thinking that you'd already looked into two good possibilities of jobs you'd like. Traveling with me would take that away from you."

"So?"

"So?" She repeated the word loudly. "It matters!"

"What matters first and foremost from now until forever is our son. This isn't going to happen without some sacrifices from both of us. You know that, Edie. Don't feel bad that I might make a few. You're making most of them."

"I'm not so sure about that."

He snorted. "Yeah, right. You're the one unwillingly grounded. You're the one with career plans that are really blowing up. I'm the lucky one. I haven't committed to any particular future yet except being the best father I can manage. That makes the rest of my choices easy."

Really? His words stuck with her the rest of the way home, and she began to wonder if he wasn't right. What if she threw everything else out the window and just thought about being the best mother possible. Would that make it easier to reach decisions?

She suspected it would. The balancing act she'd been trying to pull for months wasn't going to end with the baby's birth. As long as she felt she had to balance, instead of making one clear choice, she'd always be balancing.

As they neared the house, she said, "You don't have a computer, do you?"

"Not yet. Not while I'm remodeling."

"Then what about a bookstore?"

"We have Bea's place. What do you want?"

"It's time," she said, "to start choosing names."

Chapter Nine

Poring over a book full of baby names actually turned into a riotous afternoon. Seth was in some kind of mood and refused to get serious about it. They went through names, picking the ones that sounded absolutely awful to them, imagining some poor little boy saddled with some of them, and worse, coming up with all the possible terrible nicknames.

Edie's sides ached from laughing. It had been a while since she'd enjoyed being so silly, and Seth had a wicked wit. But just as she was beginning to think he was avoiding the entire issue with humor, and that they were getting nowhere at all, she glanced over at the pad beside him and realized he'd written down a few names.

She leaned over to read it, even as she begged him to stop making her laugh because it was beginning to hurt, and saw that he'd copied names neither of them had either willingly or unwillingly made fun of.

"Wow," she said. "We have names!"

"And we're not even halfway through the book yet," he reminded her. A smile resided in his green-brown eyes.

"Are we going to get to Seth?"

"You want to call him that?"

"Why not? Don't most people do that?"

"I don't know what most people do, but if you have two Seths around, the poor kid is probably going to be called Junior for the rest of his days."

She frowned. He had a point. "We could call him Seth Too."

"The number?"

"No." She spelled it out for him.

He snorted. "I can already hear him being called Too, and everyone thinking it *is* a number. Let's skip that idea. Names are really important. Look at my dad. I don't think his parents ever considered what calling him Nathan Tate would cause. Nate Tate? I'm sure he got a lot of double takes before everyone around here got used to it."

"I admit I wondered when I heard it. But it fits somehow."

"Sooner or later." He tapped the pad. "We've already got a few we didn't trash one way or the other. We'll have more by the time we're done. Then we can really wrangle."

He rose and went to pull a casserole out of the freezer. He pulled off the note taped to it and popped it in the oven. "From Doris Whelan, two doors down. Her prize-winning mac and cheese. From scratch, and she uses a good white cheddar. You'll like it."

"It doesn't come out of a ration box."

He laughed again, set the temperature on the oven. "An hour, she said, from frozen. Add fifteen because I didn't preheat." He taped the note to one of the few cupboard doors so he would remember where to return the dish. He'd been doing that as they ate the neighbors' bounty.

"I'm surprised so many people brought food," she said. "It must be because of you. They don't even know me."

"They don't know me all that well yet, either, but it seems to be a tradition around here. I like it."

She realized she was getting to like a lot of things about the quiet little town. Even her constant urge for action seemed to be quieting as she settled into an easier pace.

"So you had a great time flying today," he said.

She looked up, a smile coming to her lips, but the instant their eyes connected, it was as if all the air left the room. A deep certainty settled over her, not unlike that morning in Afghanistan, and she knew what was coming.

He stood there, his eyes alight with promises and hungers she still could barely imagine from their one brief coupling. Waiting. Saying nothing. Doing nothing. As if he didn't want to send her into flight. Giving her a chance to act as if she didn't feel the same thing.

But she felt it. Oh, man, she felt it. She'd been feeling it like a nagging itch since she'd set eyes on him again. Up or down, angry or laughing, the itch never went away.

It remained at the edges of her consciousness, or it burst into the foreground at surprising moments. She kept pushing it away, telling herself it was just another complication she didn't need.

Maybe she didn't need it, but she wanted it. Maybe it wasn't smart, but she didn't care anymore. All the things she had so steadfastly tried to avoid by avoiding sex had happened anyway: her career was in a shambles, her future was up in the air and she had a baby on the way.

What was there left to avoid?

Her limbs seemed to grow heavy, and heat pooled between her thighs. She rose, facing him, but unsure what to do. It had been so easy that night so long ago. So what had changed? Was it easier with a stranger than with someone you knew? That didn't make sense.

"You're so beautiful," Seth said, his voice husky. "Tell me now if I should turn off that oven."

She knew exactly what he meant, but he'd given her a graceful way to pretend she didn't understand. Her own response sounded hoarse even to her. "Turn it off."

He smiled then, an almost lazy, sleepy smile. Somehow that look ratcheted up the growing heat within her. It seemed to promise so much. Memories of their brief time together tumbled around in her head, exquisite, exciting. She knew she wanted even more this time, although she didn't know exactly what. Slow? Fast? Right now she thought she'd die if it wasn't fast and furious. Later…she hoped there *would* be a later, but at that moment she didn't care.

Now and Seth. All she wanted.

There was a click, oddly loud, as he switched the oven off. Then he slipped an arm around her waist and laid his hand on her belly. "I'll be careful."

"I don't think I'm that fragile."

"Still." The smile reached his eyes, but seemed to hold a burning intensity. She wouldn't have imagined it could feel this good, this heady, to realize a man wanted her that much. And the more so because it was Seth.

She wanted *him,* not just a man. Of that she hadn't the least doubt.

He guided her toward the stairs, then rested his hands on her hips as she climbed them ahead of him. His touch, so ordinary, nonetheless felt almost like fire through her clothes. Those flames were growing, heating her inside then turning into the most amazing ache. It far exceeded anything she had felt the last time until they were approaching culmination. Now her body was as ready to go as her mind.

At the top of the stairs, still standing behind her, he murmured, "Slowly this time. I want to appreciate you."

The whisper of his warm breath in her ear sent a thrill racing through her—his words were almost a promise.

One last sane thought tried to poke through the hot haze of desire: What was she getting into?

It vanished the instant his lips touched the side of her neck, caressing her. All of a sudden her legs felt rubbery. As if he sensed it, he swept her right off her feet, turned sideways and carried her into the bedroom. He stood her beside the bed, facing him, cupping her face and looking deep into her eyes.

"Me, too," he said, as he had on that memorable night months ago. "Me, too."

A shudder of longing ripped through her, and she tipped her head back. Never in her life had she felt more like surrendering. Never.

As he reached to lift her shirt, she muttered, "I have no waist."

"Believe me, that only makes you more beautiful. Did I tell you that you have a glow about you that you didn't before? I can't explain it."

"I was tired before."

A quiet chuckle escaped him. "Not that I noticed. This is for us, Edie. Just for *us*."

She liked the sound of that. More heat and heaviness drizzled to her core and all of a sudden she felt energized. She reached for the buttons on his shirt.

"Easy," he said.

"Like hell. There'll be time for that later."

He laughed, then granted her wish. Just as had happened months ago, clothes went flying, tossed away as fast as they could manage.

He cussed at her boots as she sat on the edge of the bed, feeling cool air whisper over her now-naked breasts. "We've really got to get you something easier," he said.

She reached out and stroked his longer hair, liking it better than the buzz cut he used to have, although that had had its charms, too. "Maybe I should never dress again."

He looked up from the boots, eyes hooded yet hot. "I could get to like that."

He finally cast the boots aside, pulled her pants off her, then reached up to cup her breasts. "They've grown," he said.

"You remember?"

"I haven't forgotten one single instant."

Talk about an inflammatory statement. She was already hot, but those words set her on fire. Every cell in her body seemed to be licked by tongues of flame.

"Hurry," she said raggedly. "Oh, damn, Seth, just hurry."

He brushed his thumbs over her nipples, more sensitive now than ever in her life, and she shivered. "Seth..."

"Oh, damn," he muttered.

The next thing she knew, she was lying back on the bed, her feet still hanging over the side, and she could feel his staff seeking entry. This, just this, would be enough. A cry escaped her as he filled her, and it felt so good she thought she would shatter.

But his hands never stopped roaming over her breasts

and belly, building the excitement in her in every way possible. She bucked a little and he responded with a deeper plunge into her.

His head bowed. First he kissed the mound of her growing baby, then his lips trailed upward, wet and hot toward her breasts. Moans started to escape her as primal needs took command.

Wanting. Needing. Hunger. Heat. The pulsing at her center spread throughout her entire body, as if she were one gigantic heartbeat. Reaching out, feeling as if she were wound tighter than a spring, she grabbed his shoulders, silently begging.

He gave her what she wanted. Leaning forward, he sucked her breasts, creating a rhythm with each movement of his mouth that kept time with her throbbing center, heightening her need until there was no thought left in her mind. With each plunge of his staff into her, she felt at once a satisfaction so deep it defied description and a rising hunger that demanded more.

The crest was close, so close. There was an agonizing moment when everything inside her seemed to still, then she peaked with a loud cry. An instant later she felt him groan and shudder, felt a new wave of heat as he jetted into her.

It could get better. Dazed, sated, she felt as light as drifting eiderdown.

A little while later, she curled against his side with her head on his shoulder and his arm around her back. He'd pulled the covers up over them and tucked a pillow under his head.

"Damn," he said, his voice full of lazy amusement, "are you helo pilots always in such a rush?"

"I thought you SEALs were the fast-in, fast-out guys."

"Only on some things." He gave her a little squeeze. "We can do that again. As often as you like. Slower, too."

"I'm not sure slower is better."

"Well, we'll find out, won't we?" He turned a little to wrap his other arm around her. "I like the baby bump. I like the changes in your body. In case you were wondering. I was crazy about you the first time, obviously, but I'm still crazy. Everything okay?"

"Never felt better."

"Me neither. Never."

There seemed to be an emphasis to the way he said it, as if he didn't want her wondering how she compared to his wives or other lovers. And it sounded like he meant it.

Warmed, she nuzzled his shoulder. "So many things I never imagined."

"Like what? Feelings?"

"Well, that, but also,...I shouldn't admit this, but I actually liked being out of control."

"Oh, sweetie, this is the best time to be out of control. You're safe with me, so let it all hang out."

"I think we just did that."

She heard the laugh rumble in his chest, temporarily muting the steady thud of his heartbeat. "That we did." Then he asked, "Are you hungry? Thirsty? I can run downstairs and grab something."

"That casserole will spoil."

"That casserole is a long way from being thawed. So, do you want anything?"

"A shower," she admitted. "Sex is sticky."

Another laugh rolled out of him. "Well, I know of this

shower only a few feet away that's plenty big enough for two. Care to join me?"

She tipped her head up until she could meet his gaze. "Why do you look so impish?"

"I have an evil side, and it's having evil thoughts about being in that shower."

Instantly she was sharing those evil thoughts. "You're on."

He tossed back the covers and led her naked to the bathroom. "Sit while I get the water warm."

So she sat on the closed commode while he turned on the two nozzles. "Extra large water heater. We can take all the time we want."

She smiled. "Why do I get the feeling you often missed showers?"

"Maybe because I did? You get so you don't pay attention. There are more important things. But I swear, the showers were the first thing I hit as soon as they were in range."

"I know."

"I'm sure you do. There we go."

He took her hand and helped her up. "You can sit on the bench if you want."

She didn't want, not yet. Instead she went into his arms, naked body pressed to naked body beneath a pounding spray of deliciously warm water. Could it get any better?

Oh, yes. As soon as they were wet, he grabbed a bottle of shampoo and began to wash her hair and massage her scalp. Relaxation poured through her, making her feel good all over.

Then he turned her under the spray to rinse her hair

and began to rub a bar of soap all over her, starting at her neck. The slick caresses were heaven, and once again heat began to pool between her thighs.

Her eyes opened. "Oh, my heavens, Seth…"

"Enjoy," he said. "Enjoy, because I sure as hell am."

She felt as if she were being worshipped. His soap-slickened hands moved everywhere, slowly and lazily, which began to build the most wonderful kind of impatient anticipation in her. She had to force herself to remain still under his ministrations, but they felt so good she was contradictorily afraid to move and put a stop to them.

Over her breasts until they tingled and her nipples hardened. Gently lifting them to wash beneath, then running his hands around to her back. More soap, more caresses, pounding warm water. Heaven on earth.

But as his hands moved lower, she found herself holding her breath. Over her hips, again and again. Closer.

She almost protested when all of a sudden he dropped down and began washing her legs from the ankles up. Instead, the hot feelings pouring through her made her grab the safety bar for support.

"Do you need to sit?" he asked instantly.

"Not yet. Please."

She thought she heard a laugh from him, but his hands never stopped moving, caressing every inch of her legs, steadily climbing, getting closer…closer…

Ah, sweet heaven. How much more could she stand?

"I told you," he said as he stood, "slow is good."

"Slow is driving me crazy."

"Exactly."

His hands slipped behind her, sliding over her bottom, then causing her to gasp as he spread her cheeks and slid his fingers between them. Who'd have thought...?

But thought ceased. Sensation took over. Damn, that felt good! A series of tremors began to pass through her, and she felt like a torch bursting into flames. Aching, wanting...

Then his soapy hands slipped around front and boldly slid between her legs.

"Ahhh..." A soft cry of sheer delight escaped her at the silky touches, first sliding over her lips, then parting them so he could touch that most sensitive knot of nerves. Over and over those gentle touches lashed her higher, bringing the pinnacle ever closer.

"Easy," he said.

"Easy?" The concept seemed foreign. What in the world did he mean?

Then his hands pulled away from her. A sound of protest escaped her but he was ruthless. He turned her under the spray, rinsing her completely.

She was just starting to feel annoyed when he urged her over to the bench.

"Sit," he said, steadying her until she was on the bench.

Now he'd wash himself, she thought and opened her eyes to watch because he was so gorgeous, even though every instinct wanted to drag him back to the bed.

He surprised her by kneeling in front of her. He pushed gently until she parted her legs.

"Slide forward just a bit," he said.

Then a whole new world opened to her as he bent his head and began licking her in her most private place. It hurt and felt so good all at once that her body tightened like a bowstring.

She felt as if she were in free fall and grabbed his shoulders as if they would steady her. But there was no steadiness now. The entire world vanished in a tsunami of passion she could never have imagined.

Up she climbed, feeling weightless in space, carried away by forces beyond her control. Surrendering and loving every moment of it.

All of a sudden he pulled his head away, drawing another cry from her, then he plunged into her, keeping his fingers between them, rubbing her nub, building the ache until it was so hard she could barely stand it.

Then came the spasms of completion, beyond anything she had yet experienced. Wave after wave of pleasure rolled through her, so strong they were almost painful.

She heard herself cry out, stars exploded behind her eyes and she shattered into a million flaming pieces.

She had no idea how long it was before she returned to her senses. She opened her eyes slowly, feeling Seth's head on her breasts, once again feeling the hot, pounding water.

She felt him pull away finally, and opened her eyes to slits. He aimed the water at her to rinse her off, then began lathering himself.

"If I thought I could stand," she mumbled, "I'd do that for you."

"Next time," he answered, winking.

She enjoyed the show anyway. He was perfect in every respect, at least as far as she was concerned. He made quick work of it, though, then insisted on drying her with a fluffy towel. She tried to help him, but she was still feeling weak for some reason.

"You need to eat. Let's get something on and go downstairs."

She put on her robe and slippers, giving him a look when he remarked that the slippers were better than her boots. He just laughed.

There she was, feeling sleepy-happy-tired from their lovemaking, and he looked full of energy. Weren't men supposed to get sleepy afterward?

Downstairs he started the casserole again, but apparently decided she needed something sooner than that. He made coffee, then offered her some slices of cheese and a quartered apple. Man, he was making her feel like a princess, cared for in all these ways.

"Milk?"

"Please." She made sure to get her requisite number of glasses each day, whether she felt like it or not. Although she supposed there was calcium in those prenatal vitamins, she'd never bothered to check how much. They didn't look big enough to have it all.

She felt so good right now it was almost frightening. She didn't know why it frightened her. Maybe because she seldom felt this good, and rarely did such feelings last.

Seth joined her at the table with fresh coffee for both of them and pulled out the baby name book. This time they didn't laugh their way through it, but discussed names more seriously while the aroma of the casserole filled the kitchen: warming cheese and some mustard. It smelled wonderful in here.

She was feeling tugs inside her that she couldn't explain. Almost like her emotions were headed in divergent directions. But she didn't want to think about that now.

Life had given her nothing of what she had just tasted and was tasting now. It was time to accept the moment for what it was and save the analysis for later. An after-action report, she thought almost wryly. She could debrief herself in the morning.

The phone rang just as they were finishing dinner. Seth answered it, saying little enough, but when he hung up he looked ruefully at her. "The whole fam-damily is on the way over."

"The what?"

"My parents. I knew I couldn't keep Mom away forever. Sorry."

Edie wondered at her lack of irritation. Then she understood. This whole family had been at the hospital when she'd had her little scare. That meant something.

"I'd better get dressed."

Seth leered at her. "Want some help?"

"Not if I want to be dressed before they get here."

His laugh followed her up the stairs.

She pulled on one of her new tops and a pair of maternity jeans. She skipped her boots, though, keeping her slippers on. She smiled to herself as she realized she didn't want them to be in the way later. Because she was certain there'd be a later.

What it all meant, she didn't know, any more than she had known what her one-night stand with him in Afghanistan meant. Certainly there had been consequences she had never imagined, but once again she had no idea what consequences might come out of this.

As she brushed her hair out she looked at herself in the mirror and wondered if she knew the real Edie. She knew the career-oriented Edie, the do-or-die officer and pilot, but the rest of her had been stunted in some way. Stunted or buried. She felt as if she were stretching out new branches, like a tree that was trying to grow.

Good or bad? Time would tell.

She reached the bottom of the stairs just as Nate and Marge Tate arrived. Marge came bearing a coffee cake, something chocolaty, and gave Edie a quick peck on the cheek. "I always wanted chocolate when I was pregnant," she said.

Nate shook her hand. "I hear you took one of the Hueys up earlier."

Edie returned his smile with a grin of her own. "It was great! I've missed flying so much."

"Probably could do quite a bit of it here, if you wanted."

She stilled, wondering if he was referring to Yuma's earlier suggestion that she work for the emergency response team. Was this some kind of family conspiracy to keep her here?

Seth didn't seem to notice. He pulled the two kitchen chairs into the living room to add seating, then went to get coffee for everyone while Marge cut and served the cake.

Edie looked at her plate as she sat in the recliner and wondered where she was going to stuff the cake. Dinner had filled her completely.

Marge sat in the other recliner, while the men took the two chairs, balancing plates on their knees and setting coffee cups on the floor.

"You really need more furniture, Seth," Marge remarked.

"I want to wait until I'm done remodeling."

"This room is done," Marge pointed out. "Just throw sheets over the furniture when you're making dust."

"Yes, Mom."

Edie saw the twinkle in his eyes, and Marge laughed. "There I go again. So have you two made any plans yet?"

Seth's face stilled. Knowing him better, as she did now, she recognized the irritation it masked. "You know, Mom," he said after a moment, "we'll deal with this in our own good time. We're working things out, okay?"

Marge looked down briefly, then gave him an almost watery smile. "I'm sorry. I'm just so concerned, that's all."

"So are we. Very. It's okay, but whatever we do has to be good for *three* people."

Nate cleared his throat. "How about them Broncos?"

The question released laughter and cleared away the tension instantly. Conversation fell into a more casual vein, with Marge chatting about the latest news from her daughters, and Nate occasionally indulging in some sports patter. Seth leaned back, a clear signal he felt they were over the rough ground.

Only once did Marge bring the conversation back to the future. "You'll come to Thanksgiving dinner, won't you?" she asked Edie. "Everyone will be there and we always have fun."

"I'll try," Edie answered uncertainly. "If I can get the time off." Thanksgiving with a whole family. Part of her wanted it, and part of her feared it.

Seth handed her a ready-made excuse if she wanted it. "It's hard to get time at the holidays, Mom," he said. "Most of the single people volunteer to cover for the people who need to get home to families."

"Oh, that's a nice thing to do," Marge answered. "But now Edie has a family, too."

Oh, boy, Edie thought, managing a weak smile.

Then, much to her later embarrassment, she actually dozed off in the chair.

Chapter Ten

She awoke as she felt her feet being lifted. She opened her eyes immediately and found Seth raising the foot of the recliner.

"Damn," he said, "I was hoping not to wake you."

"I fell asleep? Oh, my God, what must your family think? Are they still here?"

"Gone. And they think you're just one very tired pregnant lady. My mom gave me a helluva scolding for not making sure you got enough rest."

She lifted her hands to rub her eyes. "I'm so sorry. And it's not your fault."

"It sure is."

She caught the sparkle in his eyes. "Well, okay, but I don't remember objecting."

"Do you want to go up to bed? Or do you want your cake and some milk now?"

To her surprise, her appetite had returned. "The cake and milk sound great. How long was I out?"

"Maybe three hours."

Oh, man. She closed her eyes and straightened a little in her chair. The baby kicked a few times, gentle prods as he followed his own exercise routine. She smiled and rested her hand over those little poking feet or hands.

"He's moving?" Seth asked as he returned with her plate and milk.

"Always. Although he got quiet earlier." She gave him a shy smile.

"We're training him well. He needs to remember that."

Wow, that sounded like a forever kind of statement. At once she felt something tighten within her. The baby was forever, but the rest? God, it would have been so easy to make that decision, one she might rue for a very long time. How did people know these things? How did they ever make such decisions?

Seth bent and pressed his hand to her belly. When he felt the gentle pokes, he smiled. "Active little guy. Does he ever wake you?"

"Not yet. Well, except to go to the bathroom, speaking of which…"

He took everything from her and she rose to go down the hall to the half bath that looked only half-remodeled. New fixtures, but the walls still needed work. For some reason it danced across her mind that she'd like to paint it lavender. Hah! Seth would probably not love that idea.

She returned to the recliner and put her feet up. Her ankles were swelling again. "Not quite grapefruits yet," she remarked, pointing.

"That's why I decided to put your feet up. You're sure it's not a concern?"

"I asked, it's not. Not as long as it only happens in the evening after a long day. Now if I wake up with them looking huge, then I should report it."

He nodded and settled on the other recliner. "What was my dad saying about you flying a lot here?"

She hesitated. "Yuma kind of hinted that he'd like to

cut back. It sounded like he was telling me they could take me on as a pilot."

"Guess so, if Dad heard about it." He half smiled. "This county will devour you if you want. They're trying to get me on the sheriff's department. Now they want to get you on the ERT. They're good at hanging on to people they want. It's even more remarkable considering we've been going through some hard times. But take our sheriff's office, for instance."

She forked a piece of cake to her mouth. "Yes?"

"Dad took on Micah Parish, a retired buddy of his from special forces. He took on our current sheriff, Gage Dalton, former DEA. He had Yuma start up the ERT. It's always been like that. I could tell you more stories, but…they make room for people they want to keep."

"They know what kind of people they're getting that way," she suggested.

"Maybe so. However it is, take it as a compliment that Yuma hinted at that. He must have really cottoned to you."

"We sure had fun flying together."

"He certainly wouldn't have suggested it if he hadn't been impressed with your handling of the Huey. Those helos are both his babies and his nightmare."

"Nightmare?"

"Wendy told you he flew medevacs. Well, Yuma was raised a Quaker. Like a lot of the guys flying medevac, he reached a point of rage over being shot at over the wounded he was picking up. He flew in unarmed with a red cross on his fuselage. It might as well have been a target. Anyway, like a lot of others, he started carrying cases of ammunition in when he flew in to pick up the wounded. The crisis of conscience drove him to drink."

"That's awful!"

"No kidding. A pacifist turned into an ammo deliverer."

"It's different now," she remarked. "No red cross, and a good door gunner."

"War has changed. For the worst, if you ask me." His face darkened, and she left him alone with his thoughts. She was sure he'd seen and done enough to give him some black memories.

After a moment, he shook himself free of the past and managed a faint smile. "Enough of that. Yuma babies those Hueys, but I can't imagine how rough it must have been for him when he first started flying them here. For him to offer to let you pilot one is a big deal."

"I guess so." She decided it might be a good time to change the subject. She didn't need any more pressure. Big changes had turned into even bigger changes that afternoon, and they still hadn't settled enough to sort through them. "So I guess taking you on means taking the entire family?"

"Obviously." He sounded wry. "And whenever you're here, a huge chunk of the town. Everyone knows my mom and dad, and most of them know Wendy and Yuma. Think you can handle it?"

"It hasn't exactly been hard so far."

"You've barely gotten your feet wet. Still..." He shrugged. "I really like it here. Something about this place lets me shake the dust and soot off my soul."

Wow, that was an intense statement. But looking at him, she knew he meant it. He'd found peace here. How could she possibly ask him to go globe-trotting after her and their son?

But he'd offered, and he'd meant it. There had been

no mistaking the steely determination when he'd said that. This baby was going to have a father.

The only question was how much she was going to let him into *her* life. But maybe she had already breached the levy on that one. Maybe she had already let him in, possibly too far.

She sighed, realizing she was still sleepy, too sleepy for weighty analysis of anything. "I need to go to bed. I'm tired."

He didn't follow her up, but much later when she stirred in the night, she found him sleeping beside her in the bed.

Oddly, that felt comforting.

When she woke in the morning, she was disappointed to find Seth gone. Almost without thinking about it, she'd been hoping they'd make love again, but instead she heard him moving around downstairs. Probably the remodeling.

The call of nature was urgent, so she popped out of bed and headed for the bathroom. She had barely emerged when Seth reached the top of the stairs.

"Time to rise, sunshine," he said cheerfully.

"What's the rush?"

"Well, there's that walk you want to take every morning, so we need to get your physical training out of the way. Then I want to show you around some more."

He fed her a hearty breakfast of bacon, eggs and toast with juice and milk, then annoyed the hell out of her on her walk by running in circles around her.

"Typical SEAL," she said finally.

"I'm not as fast as I used to be," he admitted. "But it still feels good to run."

"Do you still weight train?"

"I haven't shown you my basement. It's one thing I finished out. My own gym. You can use it, if you want."

"Maybe I will. Walking is highly recommended, but I'd like to keep my upper body strength, within reason."

"I'll put it on the list for later."

"You have a list?"

"Of course. Every day needs a plan." Then he winked and she couldn't help chuckling.

She caught sight of the mountains to the west and paused. The air was so clear this morning they looked close enough to touch. "Remember all that snow in Afghanistan?" she said suddenly. "Like that day I picked you up?"

"They have hellacious winters."

"What about here?"

"Cold but not nearly as snowy. We're actually a pretty dry climate for the most part. Although that seems to be changing like so much about the weather. Why?"

"Just wondering. The mountains reminded me."

"Our mountains are pretty craggy in places, but not nearly as hostile, at least not around here. We'll take our son camping up there sometime. It's great."

Making more plans. Uneasiness trickled through her but she pushed it away. Things were moving too fast. Maybe. But at least one thing was coming fast regardless: motherhood. And there were still so many things to decide.

"We need to talk," she said finally.

"Hence driving around the county later. Neutral territory. No distractions in the form of your lovely body."

That warmed her all the way to her toes, but she managed a snort. "You've got your mind on one thing."

"Not really. But for safety's sake, we'll take a drive. And if you give me that sidelong look again, you may not finish your walk."

She had to laugh. "Sure, you're going to pick me up and carry me back to the house in plain view of the entire world...."

"Don't tempt me, because I can and I will."

She looked at him again and saw no humor in his face. Steely determination once again. Sometimes she could definitely see the man who had been a SEAL for so long. Not a person to screw around with.

God, a SEAL. Had she really been foolish enough to get involved with one of the most dangerous men on earth? Nice as he was to her, he would always be the guy who could go solo, or with a team, into impossibly dangerous situations. A guy who wouldn't hesitate no matter how high the risks.

"Will the real Seth Hardin stand up?" she muttered.

Suddenly his hand gripped her elbow. "Let's go take that drive now."

"I haven't finished my walk."

"We can finish it later."

"What's the damn rush, Seth?"

"I get the feeling that you're busy looking for reasons to wash your hands of me. So let's get acquainted. For real."

"We can do that while we walk."

"Not if we get into a shouting match. Excuse me, but I don't want half the town hearing our business."

She couldn't argue with that. He was looking awfully grim all of a sudden, and she didn't want to argue with him, either.

Was he right? Was she trying to find some reason,

any reason, to discard him? Because he was a SEAL and SEALs were dangerous men? Because she couldn't quite believe he was the nice guy she'd spent the past couple of weeks with? The amazingly tender lover?

She said nothing as he helped her into the car, nothing as he stopped by Maude's to pick up some kind of lunch, and then they were driving out into the gently rolling countryside that seemed so empty, but must have been full of ranches and farms. He didn't speak, either. He seemed to be mulling something and his jaw was tight.

At last he pulled off the road and drove over a bumpy track to a stand of cottonwoods beside a stream. "I know the guy who owns this place," he said tautly. "He won't mind. But we may see some sheep."

She didn't answer because she didn't know how to answer. How had such a stupid little remark on her part opened this all up in some way she couldn't begin to imagine? What were they dealing with here?

He pulled a blanket from the trunk and spread it on the ground for her to sit on in the shade of autumn leaves, with the stream burbling gently nearby. Under other circumstances, it would have been idyllic.

He remained standing, facing the stream and the mountains, his back to her.

"You want to know the real Seth Hardin?" he finally asked.

"I'm not sure what I meant by that."

He faced her. "I know what you meant. So I'm going to tell you. I'm an assassin, a person who killed simply because I had orders to. I blew up buildings. I fought bad guys in places you've never heard of as part of covert operations. I took on gangs of pirates to save ship crews. I've even boarded ships at sea in the dead of night to prevent the transport of nuclear materials or weapons. I've gone in undercover and spied. I have taken lives with my bare hands. I am a SEAL. That will always be with me. Is that what scares you?"

She stuck out her chin. "Did I say I was scared?"

He leaned slightly toward her. "I can also read people very well because my life has depended on it. You don't need to say it."

"Seth…"

"Let me finish. I'm the guy they make movies about without telling the whole ugly story. I'm capable of all those things and I have to live with it. But I've made peace with my past. The Seth Hardin you've met here, and that night in Afghanistan, is also the real Seth Hardin. He's the man I want to be all the time now that I don't have to war anymore. Both sides are equally real. But it's not me you're really scared of."

"What?" Startled, she almost gaped.

He put his hands on his hips. "If you remember, I gave you my contact information that morning. I made it as possible as I could for you to find me anywhere in the world through my parents. You didn't give me a damn thing."

Now her jaw did drop.

"I actually *hoped* you would get in touch. I wanted to see you again. Never thought of that, did you? No, of course not. You made an assumption and walked away and tried to never take another look back. You wanted to erase the whole thing from your life."

"But…"

"Yeah, but. Instead, life grabbed you and wouldn't let you pretend it never happened. You came here out of some sense of duty, hoping like hell I'd tell you to kiss off. Well, shock, lady, I don't want you to kiss off and I am not going to give up my son. So maybe you need to knit your head together and figure out what the hell is frightening you. What are *you* scared of, because it sure as hell isn't me, however much you try to make it your excuse."

He paused a moment, while she struggled with the bombardment, scrambling for a place from which she could start thinking.

"One other thing," he said. "I still have nightmares occasionally. Once in a while I remember things I'd rather not. But I was damned lucky. I got out of all that reasonably intact. So, any way you want to slice it, I am not a threat to you, and I am not a threat to that baby. Unless you decide I am, and that all comes back to what *you* are afraid of."

Then he turned and strode away along the stream, leaving her with the sounds of rustling leaves and the stream. A dead leaf slowly drifted down and she watched it fall.

She wanted to yell after him, to tell him to come back, to tell him he was all wrong. But somewhere deep inside the truth had sunk home. *She* was afraid. But of what?

Tiredness was creeping up on her again, maybe from the tension, but she didn't want to give in. She had to think. She *had* to. This was too important. He was right, there was their son to consider. If for no other reason she had to figure out why she kept getting the urge to run, yet felt an equally strong urge to stay.

She thought she'd been sorting things out so well when she'd driven out here, but clearly there were a whole bunch of issues she hadn't even taken into account.

Like him giving her his family's address and phone

number. She'd tossed it like trash, never considering why he'd given it to her. Never thinking that he really might want to see her again. Not wanting even to admit the possibility.

All that stuff about her career and not damaging it was beginning to sound pretty thin even to her. Oh, yeah, she had meant it, but it was still only half a life. A good life, but only half. Other officers, other pilots, got married and had families. She could have done it without ruining anything. Hell, for all she knew, it might have helped her because the air force was big on that whole family thing.

Instead she had chosen to live like a cloistered nun, even avoiding most of the ordinary socializing. Oh, she did what was expected of her, but she avoided the casual stuff, keeping her friendships at work and the rest of her life fairly empty. She had called it focus, but now she wondered why.

Finally she lay back, cradling her head on her hands and staring up into the gently stirring leaves. She could see a deep blue sky beyond them, a sky she loved to fly in.

She'd been frightened of losing her ability to fly. She knew that. She'd been miserable since her removal from flight status. But it was more than that. Much more.

Slowly, cautiously, she opened her well of memories, delving all the way back to her childhood. There had to be something somewhere to explain the driven, single-minded woman she had become. Something that frightened her. Or maybe something she feared becoming.

Half an hour later Seth returned. He wasn't happy with the way he'd broached his concerns, wasn't pleased with his own behavior, but with Edie he felt sometimes like he was banging his head on a brick wall. They'd take a few steps forward and then he'd watch that internal retreat of hers.

Yes, it was all new. Yes, it was happening fast, but the bottom line hadn't changed one bit. Nothing would deter him from being a father to his son. Nothing. So they had to get past that wall of hers to some kind of decent agreement.

When he found her asleep, he wrapped the other half of the blanket over her and sat on the grass, staring at the mountains. It was cool today, and while the blanket and her jacket would be enough for a while, he worried about her getting a chill if she slept too long.

But he didn't wake her. Damn, he'd come on like gangbusters, but he wasn't used to pulling his punches and dancing around things. He knew who he was. In fact, he suspected he knew himself far better than she knew herself.

Something was going on inside of her that wasn't making any sense, at least not to him, and he suspected not to her. Not good.

In four months they'd be parents. They *had* to find an accommodation of some kind. He'd marry her tomorrow under any terms she wanted, he'd simply travel with her, married or not, or he'd visit that kid every damn weekend. No way was he giving that boy up.

So she'd better agree to something. And she'd better figure out what kept pulling her back every time she moved closer. After what they'd shared yesterday, nothing could have appalled him more than to sense the fear in her while they were out walking. It was another round in a boxing match where his opponent was invisible, not only to him, but also to her he guessed.

They sure needed a more stable arrangement than that, for their own sakes but most especially the baby's. Kids were so sensitive to tensions. He'd learned that from his nieces and nephews. They had built-in radar for an upset parent.

As he watched Edie sleep, he felt an unwanted wave of tenderness, something he hadn't felt often in his life except with his wives. And nothing quite this strong, maybe because a baby had never been involved before.

Hell, he'd been hard on her and probably should apologize. She had reasons to be dubious. Hadn't he himself called his father and asked him how men like them transitioned to fatherhood?

Everything in his life had trained him in a way that hardly seemed likely to create a good father. Fatherhood would require a whole different set of mental and emotional muscles, and he was sure some of them had been stunted by training and experience.

Could he nurture them fast enough, well enough?

Maybe he should trust Edie's concerns about him. They shared a lot of experience, but despite all the risks she had taken and the dangers she had flown into, she hadn't visited the same dark boxes of the human mind and soul. She probably had every right to be worried about him.

He looked away toward the mountains again, asking himself questions, searching deep inside, trying to measure himself against the father who had raised him and the father he had found later. Could he really live up to that? He was determined to, and there was very little he made up his mind to do that he hadn't accomplished.

But this was different. Was having two good examples enough?

One thing he was sure of, he couldn't afford to mess this up. Edie and their baby were too important. Lives were at stake, as simple as that. Futures.

This was, without a doubt, the most important undertaking of his entire life.

"Seth?"

Edie's sleepy voice reached him. She was still curled up with the blanket wrapped around her. At once he stretched out beside her on the grass, looking into her drowsy face.

"I'm here. Are you getting cold?"

"A tiny bit, but I'm fine." Those blue eyes opened, still drowsy. "I'm sorry I made you mad."

"You didn't really make me mad. I think you scared me."

A tiny smile curved her lips. "You? Scared?"

"I have an intimate acquaintance with fear at all levels and of all kinds. A frequent companion."

"Well, I'm sorry."

"I'm sorry, too, for coming on like gangbusters. You need time, and you have every right to work things through."

"I'm beginning to wonder if I've been working through all the wrong things." She sighed. Her eyes drooped closed, then slowly opened again. "I'm thinking, Seth. I promise I'm thinking. About myself. About what exactly I'm doing and why. You made a good point."

He shook his head a little. "I've got no business analyzing you."

"Sure you do. I'm the mother of your son."

With amazement, he felt his heart squeeze. "Yes, you are. And I'm glad you are."

She sighed. "Dang, I'm hungry again. I can't believe it. And I need the facilities. Again."

His mood lifted a bit. "I know a great tree. And lunch is in the car. Or we can head home and get you warm."

She surprised him then, seizing his hand for the first time to pull it beneath the blanket and press it to her belly. She'd never done that before. She smiled. "He's happy."

Seth sure as hell hoped so, but he started smiling, too, as he felt the little prods. "How impatient are you?"

"Not terribly yet. It's still a long way. But others have told me the last month will seem endless."

"I can imagine."

She opted for the tree, obviously, but also decided to have a picnic lunch. "It's beautiful here. I hope we can come again sometime."

Well, that was a change, he thought, feeling lighter yet. This was her first mention of something she wanted to do with him down the road. A good sign? Maybe they were getting over the first hump? Which still left some mountains to climb, he reminded himself. In fact, a whole damn range of them.

The day began to grow colder, so shortly after they finished their sandwiches, they headed back to town. He asked if she wanted to do something, but she shook her head.

"I've got some heavy-duty thinking to do."

And that's what she did. She withdrew to some place inside herself, sitting in the recliner or going out to walk alone. Leaving him wondering what the hell was in the offing. At least she wasn't packing her duffel.

Yet.

* * *

Edie had no intention of packing her duffel, although she had little idea what decisions she was going to make about everything else. Reaching all the way back in her memory, she tried to figure out how she had gotten to this point. She needed to figure it out for the sake of her son. How could she be a good mother if she didn't know what fears were holding her back?

Because Seth was right about that. She wasn't afraid of him. Not as if he were some kind of threat to the baby. It had nothing to do with him being a SEAL, but everything to do with some part of her.

She didn't have to think very hard about the obstacles. She knew she was a control freak. She'd committed to only two things in her life: the air force and CSAR. Big commitments, but very much under her control.

She couldn't control Seth, and all too soon she wouldn't be able to control the baby, either. But why did she feel that need to be in charge, to be able to handle so much of life with surety and a plan?

Yeah, she could roll with the punches. She'd had to on many occasions, but there was always that sense of control, of knowing she could deal with the unexpected that came up on a mission.

This was very different. A whole new world. Life had begun throwing curveballs, and they just kept coming. Worse, the curveballs involved other people. You might be able to control most of what happened with a mechanical failure or a weather problem, or even when being shot at, but you couldn't control other people. Ever.

Which made all of this one big scary unknown.

So yeah, she was afraid. Of herself. Of the future. Of

not having an ironclad plan. And how silly to think she could have made one that would last any length of time.

Seth had pointed out a couple of times that she kept threatening to run. She couldn't deny it. She kept wanting to go back to her familiar world, however messed up it was at the moment.

She sat on a park bench during one of her long walks the next day, trying to sort out a whole bunch of feelings, trying to find their source. Seth had been giving her space, even to the point of sleeping in the other room, but so far she had gotten nowhere useful.

What was it she *really* feared?

The lack of control or something else?

Abandonment.

The word floated up out of her subconscious and froze her as if a spike had just driven into her mind.

Abandonment.

She jumped up from the bench and started walking as fast as she could without making herself too breathless. Evidently it disturbed the baby because she felt a couple of serious kicks, so she slowed down a little.

"No." She spoke aloud to herself. Not that. Really?

The day was beginning to darken, but she ignored it, determined to fight this demon, whether imagined or real.

She'd been living a long time with the fact that her mother had left to sink into a world of drug addiction and eventually death. There was nothing there she hadn't been dealing with for a long time, and she knew how lucky she had been to have a grandmother who had loved her and cared for her.

But then her grandmother had died. Well, elderly people die, right? Surely that hadn't added to her sense of abandonment.

Her insides clenched a little as she looked at herself through this new lens. True? Not true? Had she somehow developed some ridiculous notion that everyone she cared about would leave her sooner or later, so it was wise not to care?

Look at Seth. He'd lost two wives, but he was prepared to jump in with both feet for this baby. Surely, he had lost buddies and friends as she had. He hadn't turned it into some kind of psychological trauma. He still had made deep connections with his new family. Nor was he running from this child, which must have landed in his lap like an unexpected grenade. No, he was committed even to the point of entering into a loveless marriage for the sake of their son.

Damn. He hadn't wavered. She was the one doing all the wavering, but she sure as hell was the one who was going to deliver a baby in four months and become a mother for the rest of her days, not a job that could be shirked or evaded. Not unless she wanted to be like her mother.

Once again she froze, midstep. Like her mother?

Confusion swamped her for a minute. Like her mother? No way was she like her mother. She'd already decided to keep this child and raise it the best way she could manage. No, she would not abandon her baby.

But she had resented some of the sacrifices she would have to make. Had that roused her fears that she might fail? Or was the fear something else?

She realized she was close to the Tates' house and, for a second, just a second, considered stopping to talk to Marge. But Marge had her own agenda, and had experienced all of this under a very different set of circumstances. Talking with her might be more confusing than helpful, and anyway, she needed to reach her own answers and conclusions.

Turning, she traced her steps back to Seth's. If abandonment was her real issue, she didn't have a foggy idea of how to deal with it. Nor did she have any idea how to address it with Seth. There were some promises people could make, with the best of intentions, but no guarantees they'd be able to keep them.

There lay the entire crux of the matter. For a risk-taker, she was showing herself to be one hell of a coward.

Warm lights shone through the windows as she approached the house. When she opened the front door, delicious aromas filled the air, emanating from the kitchen. She followed them and found Seth making a salad while something baked in the oven.

"Smells wonderful," she said.

He turned with a smile. "Baked ziti. I may even be able to manage garlic bread. Take a seat. Coffee? Milk?"

"Coffee," she said as she sat and slipped her jacket off.

He didn't question her, didn't press her. He just brought her the coffee and remarked that he could feel the chill all around her. "Need a blanket?"

"I'll be fine in just a minute. I didn't get that cold."

"Well, we do know the cold, don't we?"

Remembering Afghanistan, she knew he was right. It really got cold up in those mountains. She wondered how many nights he'd endured in those frigid temperatures and the deep snow, but didn't ask. Redacted.

But she liked the way he said *we*. It sounded especially good, coming from him.

"Do you need a nibble? Dinner won't be ready for about forty-five minutes."

"Apple?" she asked.

"Coming up."

So common, so ordinary, so casual. So damn normal, even while she could almost feel the storm hovering overhead. Good storm or bad storm she didn't know, but until decisions were made, conclusions reached, that black cloud would continue to hover.

She ate half the apple before she spoke, while he finished the salad and started putting garlic butter on a baguette.

"I've been thinking," she said.

His answer sounded light, although she thought she saw tension tighten his shoulders. "I gathered that."

"I told you I'm a control freak."

"I'd be surprised if you weren't, given what you do. I pretty much am, too, I guess."

"Maybe. But I think with me it isn't a trained response."

He turned from buttering the bread to face her. "No?"

"No." She stared at the apple. "One word surfaced, one I hadn't thought about."

"Which is?"

"Abandonment."

"That's heavy."

She dared to glance at him and found him both waiting and watchful. But there was something more there. He didn't appear to be a man poised for trouble. No, he looked a bit…sad?

"I guess," she said. "I can't figure it. I've been dealing with my mother's desertion since I was old enough to know. My grandmother's death was…well, hardly unexpected for a woman of her years. We all lose people we know in combat. So why an abandonment issue?"

He gave a little questioning shake of his head, but didn't say anything.

"I mean, if anyone could have an issue like that, it would be you. You knew your whole life you were adopted."

"True. If I had an issue with it, I don't remember it. But I couldn't tell you why."

"I know. And I can't tell you why I do. It's just sitting there in the basement of my subconscious. It's like a land mine waiting to be stepped on or something. I don't know. I just know that I've only made two commitments in my adult life, and they were both to my job."

"That bothers you?"

"It should. It does. But that's why I kept threatening to leave. I'm safe in the air force, safe in my job. The rules are all clear-cut, the plans laid out and the air force won't abandon me. Or at least they didn't until I became pregnant."

"They still haven't," he said quietly.

"Maybe not. But this new future I'm facing…" She shrugged and pushed the plate and apple away. "No guarantees. No plans. No reliability. The only thing I'm sure of is that I'm going to have a child to care for, and I don't even know if I'll be a good mother. How the hell would I begin to know how?"

He came to her then, kneeling on the hard floor beside her chair and wrapping his arms around her. "Everybody starts out knowing very little about being a parent. It's on-the-job training for most of us. But I think you have everything it takes, and you're smart enough to learn what you need."

"I sure hope so." She sighed, then leaned toward him a bit to rest her forehead on his shoulder. "I'm sorry I've been ignoring you since yesterday."

"I got that heavy stuff was going on. I'm not totally dense."

She gave a weak laugh. "You're not dense at all. But all this brings us back to what's right for this baby."

"And for us," he reminded her. "What's right for both of us matters, too. I've been pretty insistent about being a father to this child. I mean it. But you have to be happy with the terms, too. I was thinking yesterday that a whole lot of tension between the two of us wouldn't be a good thing for our son, either. So we work that out somehow. Anything short of telling me to get lost or visit only twice a year."

She shook her head slightly against his shoulder. "That would be cruel to both of you. I'm not going there. I'm not even thinking about it anymore. No, we need something more stable."

"Agreed. And you're still feeling cold to me. How about I get you some more coffee or hot cocoa or something, and we eat? Important discussions are better when people aren't cold, tired and hungry."

He paused. "I'd suggest a hot shower, but that would likely cause us to ruin dinner, and this is my first attempt at baked ziti. I expect rave reviews."

The strange sadness that had been filling her lifted, and she managed a laugh as he pulled away to finish dinner preparations.

"I do have one funny thing to tell you," he said as he sprinkled some grated parmesan on the split loaf of bread. "Mom called wanting to know if we'd made plans yet. I told her that I'd asked you for a marriage of convenience and was awaiting your answer."

Edie clapped her hand to her mouth, torn between laughter and horror. "Seth, you didn't!"

"I did." He turned and gave her a devilish look. "I must say, I had the rare pleasure of rendering my mother speechless."

"Oh. My…" Laughter won the day, and before she knew it, it tumbled out of her until she had to wrap her arms around herself. "Oh, Seth, you're terrible."

"I'm also a lot of fun. She'll get over it."

Edie wiped at her eyes and tried to catch her breath. "I almost stopped to talk to her a little while ago. I'm glad I didn't. Can you just imagine?"

"It would have been a toss-up between raking me over the coals or pressuring you to accept. I can't decide which. So yeah, it's good you didn't stop."

Another thought had been occurring to her increasingly over the past day, but she kept it to herself while they ate. Thinking about the environment in which she wanted to raise this child…well, it had made her look at some things straight on. But they could talk later.

The ziti was wonderful, as were the bread and salad, and she spared no praise.

"Keep talking like that and I'll cook for you every night," he said finally.

"You're welcome to it. Not my thing, I don't think."

"I'm discovering I like it."

After they cleaned up and put the leftovers away, they retired to the living room, him with coffee, her with cocoa. She struggled with her boots and finally Seth pushed her hands away and did it for her. "I swear," he said, "I am taking you shoe shopping tomorrow. No arguments."

She offered none, because it kind of tickled her in some silly way.

"Want me to go get your slippers?"

"My socks will work for now." She leaned back, putting her feet up. "This feels so good."

"Yeah, it does," he agreed.

She couldn't read his face again, but she sensed he meant more than putting his feet up.

"So," she said finally.

"Yes?"

"I've been thinking about my abandonment issues. And about something else."

"What's that?"

"Have you seen base family housing since it was turned over to private contractors?"

"Not really."

"It's pretty bad. I keep hearing stories about how it's moldy and unsafe. One woman I work with had to move her family out on doctor's orders."

"That's not good. But there are places off base."

"Of course. But that's just the start of what I was thinking."

"I'm all ears."

"Being here all this time has been a good thing. It gave me a comparison." She bit her lower lip. "Do I want to raise a military brat who'll move every couple of years, or do I want my child to have a stable home in a familiar environment, friends he can keep his whole life?"

"Interesting question."

She noted he didn't offer an opinion. She was walking out onto this limb by herself. Maybe that was a good thing. Maybe not.

"Anyway, I think growing up here would be better for him."

For an instant she saw that amazing stillness in him. Then he asked, "Are you proposing leaving him with me?"

"Not exactly."

At that he put his feet on the floor and leaned forward. "Would you be part of this?"

"That's what I'm thinking."

He stood and began to pace. "Your career, Edie. That's everything to you."

"It's not everything. It was wrong of me to make it everything, and now I have something else on the way that's even more important. I realized that. Yes, you can raise a child in the military, and lots of people do it very well, even though those long absences and worries can take a toll. But I have a choice, and how much better if I give our son a hometown and a whole fam-damily, as you call it."

He stopped to face her. "It's not all Currier and Ives."

"I didn't think it was. I watch you tussle with your mother. I'm sure people here are like people everywhere. But whatever the problems, I'd rather our son not be rootless."

After a moment he nodded slowly. "I can't exactly disagree."

"Seth, I don't want my kid, *our* kid, to grow up with a feeling of abandonment. With a reluctance to make connections that won't last. I can't say for sure that would happen if I stayed on active duty, but I can say for damn near sure it won't if I don't."

"But that would kill you!"

"It won't kill me. Even less if Yuma meant what he said about flying for the ERT. But it's all about this baby. It only struck me around the time I arrived here that I was trying to fit this baby into my life and that maybe I had it exactly backward. I need to fit my life around this baby. Isn't that what you're willing to do?"

"It's not exactly the same."

"Really? You were prepared to become a camp follower, and I don't think that was your plan, either, before I showed up."

He remained silent. Damn, she wished she could read him right now. Sometimes his face could turn into a carved statue. Her heart had accelerated with nervousness, and she wanted so desperately to know how he was really feeling. But evidently he had decided that it was her time to talk.

Finally he asked, very quietly, "What about the rest, Edie? What about you and me?"

"I don't want a marriage of convenience."

"Oh. So you get a house up the street?"

She hesitated. "Seth... If necessary."

"If necessary? What the hell does that mean?"

She couldn't bring herself to tell him. She already felt as exposed as a raw nerve ending. Defenseless. Without protection. And now he was going to get mad?

"You're waffling," he said flatly. "Hesitating. Edie, if there's one thing I want from you, it's some certainty about what you're doing and what you want. It's not like you to not speak your mind, and I need that right now. Where do I stand? Where do you stand? Please."

Her throat tightened, things inside her started crumbling. Where had this woman come from, because she sure wasn't the woman she had been when she arrived here. "I want…" She could barely squeeze the words out. "I told you about my issue with…abandonment."

He swore. She might have jerked back except that she didn't have time. He scooped her up from the chair and headed for the stairs.

"We're going to settle this," he said grimly. "Now. I told you I was a lousy pussyfooter."

She felt on the verge of tears. She was scared of her own vulnerability, and maybe that had been her worst fear all along. Fear that if she ever let down her walls she could be hurt again.

He laid her on the bed, then undressed her as gently as if she were a child. She could barely see through the dampness in her eyes, through the tears that didn't fall. The next thing she knew, he was naked under the covers with her, his legs and arms wrapped around her, holding her as close as he could get her. As close as two people could get physically. She felt surrounded by him, and oddly that made her feel safe.

"I. Will. Never. Abandon. You." He spoke each word separately and distinctly, emphasizing each. "Do you hear me?"

"Yes," she whispered brokenly.

"I mean it, Edie. I swear it. I will never abandon you. If you want me gone, you're going to have to tell me to get lost, because otherwise I will never, ever, leave you."

"But that's not fair to you," she protested, even as the terror in her heart tried to ease.

"Yes, it is. Because I don't want to be anywhere else. Period. Ever."

"But how can you possibly be sure of that?"

"First of all, I keep my word. But there's this other thing, too."

"Which is?"

"It's called a leap of faith. I took it every time I departed on a mission, and so did you. Admit it. There's only so much you can know, only so much you can plan for. After that you're going on faith. Faith that you can deal. Faith that you'll find a way. No matter how much we try to control it, most of life is one great big risk, one great big leap of faith. Hell, every single one of us takes a leap of faith every time we get behind the wheel of a car."

He paused. "I took a leap of faith both times I married."

"That should tell you something."

"Actually, what it taught me is that nothing good ever comes without a risk. With Darlene, the risk went sour. With Maria, life just happened. A drunk driver at the wrong place at the wrong time. But there was a helluva lot of happiness in the meantime. I don't regret either decision."

"Really?" She lifted her eyes to meet his gaze and saw certainty unshadowed by pain.

"Where do you get without taking risks, Edie? You don't need me to tell you."

She closed her eyes, trying not to let his closeness distract her from the issues. She would have loved to cast all the questions to the wind and forget them in some incredible lovemaking, but that would merely postpone the more important concerns. Time was getting short. Before she knew it, her leave would be over. Before she knew it, she'd have a baby. Some things could wait no longer.

"I... Seth, you don't really want a loveless marriage.

You've already had two marriages for love. How could you settle for less?"

"Ahh."

Something in the tone of his voice alerted her, and she snapped open her eyes to see his smiling face only inches away. "Loveless marriage," he repeated.

"Yes. A marriage of convenience. You said it yourself."

"I'd settle for it, if that were the case. But I don't think that's it."

"No? Then what is?"

"Edie, do you love me?"

She froze for an instant, her mind scrambling around like a mouse looking for escape. Finally, the words burst from her. "How the hell would I know? I've never been in love!"

He rolled her gently onto her back, propping himself over her on his elbows, one leg still thrown across hers. "Love is something you feel and something you do, not something you define. But what really worries you is that I might not love you. Isn't it?"

She faced the stark terror then. His question drove it to the core of her entire being. "I need to trust," she said weakly.

"You already trust me or we wouldn't be here right now. Trust isn't the issue, Edie. You're afraid of what you feel for me, afraid that I could hurt you with it."

There it was, printed in large font in brilliant full color on the forefront of her brain. He could hurt her. He could hurt her worse than anyone in her entire life, including mountain guerillas armed with RPGs. Worse than her mother's abandonment of her, worse than her grandmother's death.

She felt a hot tear roll down one cheek and forced herself to meet his gaze. "I'm terrified," she admitted.

"I know you are." He shifted, cupping her face between his hands. "I've been terrified for a while that you'd disappear when I wasn't looking. I promised I won't abandon you. Now I'm going to tell you something else. I won't hurt you, not in any real way. Oh, everybody messes up and causes some unhappiness from time to time, but I would never *really* hurt you."

"How can you be sure?"

"Because I love you."

The words sank in slowly, reaching tensions deep within her, beginning to dissolve the fear. "How do you know? I don't get how you know!"

"Because I know how much it would hurt to lose you. How much I need to see your face every day, to hold you in my arms every night. I know how badly you could hurt me. Trust me, I know."

He probably knew better than anyone, she thought. He slid over her, filling her with his hardened staff, uniting them into one. But he didn't move, even as a sigh of pleasure escaped her.

"I know I love you. And I don't care if it takes twenty years for you to be sure you feel the same about me. I'll be there."

She thought about the years ahead, tried to imagine them without Seth, and couldn't. The mere thought of it hurt her deep inside.

Was that how you figured it out, by knowing life without a particular person would be unendurable? Because life without Seth looked like a lunar landscape to her now, barren and without air. Colorless.

She struggled under the blankets, and at last managed

to reach up and caress his shoulders. "I can't live without you anymore," she admitted. "I hated feeling that way."

"And now?"

"Now I think I love it."

He smiled and began to move slowly inside her. Gently. "We'll go back to Minot together. You can resign after the baby is born. Yuma will be thrilled because he's been pressing me to push you into taking over his job."

"Is that why we're getting married? For Yuma?"

"Hell no," he said, just before he kissed her. "We're getting married because life won't be worth living any other way." Suddenly he lifted his head. "But let's not tell my mom yet."

"Why?"

"Because I want to make the announcement to everyone at Thanksgiving."

Before she could answer, he kissed her again and buried himself deeper.

A long time later she said the words he wanted to hear, because she was finally absolutely certain.

"I love you, Seth."

Her heart took off for the heavens, soaring with joy and an amazing freedom. Judging by the look on his face, so did his.

She felt she would never touch ground again.

Epilogue

Edie stood at the sliding glass doors in the family room of the Tates' house. Behind her swirled an unbelievably big family—six daughters, six husbands, eight grandchildren, plus Seth and the Tates. Thanksgiving dinner still filled her stomach, which had grown noticeable over the past few weeks. Outside, night darkened the world and snow covered the ground, but inside everything was warm as the family discussed putting up the Christmas tree the next day.

So many people. She had been trying all day to connect names and faces, but it didn't seem to matter to anyone. They welcomed her warmly, as if she had always belonged, and happiness settled into her heart.

She had made the right decision. She wanted her son to grow up in this family, to be part of their many Thanksgivings and Christmases to come.

Arms slipped around her from behind and she smiled.

"Overwhelmed?" Seth asked.

"A little. But it's great."

"Do you need to rest or are you ready to make our announcement?"

She turned within the circle of safety his arms provided. Tipping her head back, she kissed him. "I'm ready."

"Okay. Want me to do the honors?"

"It's your family."

His smile widened and he dropped a kiss on the tip of her nose. "Okay." He turned, keeping one arm around her, and raised his voice. "Hey, everybody. I have an announcement."

It took a few minutes, mostly to get the kids settled. Edie felt almost embarrassed to have everyone staring at her.

"Here's the thing. Most of you already know from Mom that I'm going to be a father. And I can't think of a better time to tell you all how happy I am about that than Thanksgiving, because I'm incredibly thankful. In fact, I'm thrilled. But I'm even more thankful because Edie has agreed to marry me."

The applause was instantaneous. Marge clapped her hands to her face and began to laugh and cry at the same time.

Everyone started to move toward them, but Seth held up his hand. "I am so very, very grateful that this woman came into my life." He looked down into Edie's face. "I am so grateful for a failure that has turned into the best thing in my life, ever."

He bent to kiss her. The room started moving toward them and a small voiced piped up.

"Is Uncle Seth a Thanksgiving Daddy?"

He lifted his head, holding Edie's eyes with his. "I sure am, Billy. I sure am."

* * * * *

A sneaky peek at next month...

Cherish™

ROMANCE TO MELT THE HEART EVERY TIME

My wish list for next month's titles...

In stores from 15th November 2013:

☐ Snowflakes and Silver Linings — Cara Colter

& Snowed in with the Billionaire — Caroline Anderson

☐ A Cold Creek Noel & A Cold Creek Christmas
   Surprise — RaeAnne Thayne

In stores from 6th December 2013:

☐ Second Chance with Her Soldier — Barbara Hannay

& The Maverick's Christmas Baby — Victoria Pade

☐ Christmas at the Castle — Marion Lennox

& Holiday Royale — Christine Rimmer

Available at WHSmith, Tesco, Asda, Eason, Amazon and Apple

Just can't wait?

Visit us Online
You can buy our books online a month before they hit the shops! **www.millsandboon.co.uk**

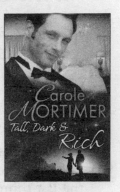

Come home this Christmas to Fiona Harper

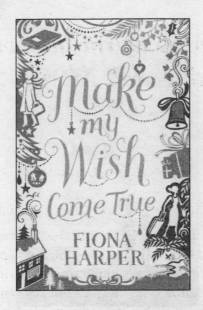

From the author of *Kiss Me Under the Mistletoe* comes a Christmas tale of family and fun. Two sisters are ready to swap their Christmases—the busy super-mum, Juliet, getting the chance to escape it all on an exotic Christmas getaway, whilst her glamorous work-obsessed sister, Gemma, is plunged headfirst into the family Christmas she always thought she'd hate.

www.millsandboon.co.uk

She's loved and lost — will she ever
learn to open her heart again?

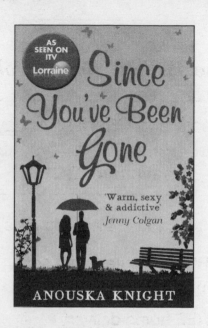

B.